PRAISE FOR

Praise for **The Norsewomen Series**:

"...The Norse Queen is an absorbing tale of sacrifice and courage. ...I was riveted to the pages as each character fought against the constraints Gudrød bound them both with. The characters are complex and compelling...

"Based on the real-life historical figure of Queen Asa, Wittenberg's thorough and detailed research paints a vivid picture of early medieval Viking life...This is a fascinating glimpse into what a strong woman's life in Viking times might have looked like, and I eagerly anticipate more from Wittenberg's The Norsewomen series."

--**Editor's Choice** –Historical Novels Review

"...This is a Scandinavian saga. Well-written, with a significant number of strange, ancient Norse words, handled with such dexterity by the author that they are easily assimilated and barely affect the flow of the story...**Highly recommended**.

--Discovering Diamonds

"…Wittenberg has a comfortable grasp on Viking culture, from practices preparing food for winter, weaponry and warcraft, as well as ship construction and repair. The varied women's roles and their training as shield maidens are some of my favorite aspects of the series… The characters and time period come alive within Wittenberg's prose, casting a spell on all who enter the halls of the Norsewomen series."

--Review of *The Falcon Queen* for Historical Novels Review

"The Norse Queen brims with action in a world both exhilarating and terrifying, peopled with sorceresses, warring jarls, and even shape-shifters. In its tale of one woman's steadfast courage in the face of tragedy, it gives life and breath to a long-forgotten 9th century queen."

--Patricia Bracewell, Author of *Shadow on the Crown* and *The Price of Blood*

"A journey back into the heart and soul of ancient Viking realms. Queen Åsa of Tromøy, a true historical figure almost lost in the mists of time, returns to vivid life in "The Norse Queen." Step inside a Scandinavian saga in all its richness. If you love "Beowulf" you will also love "The Norse Queen

--Margaret George, NYT Bestselling Author

THE RAIDER BRIDE

BOOKS BY JOHANNA WITTENBERG

The Norsewomen Series

The Norse Queen

The Falcon Queen

The Raider Bride

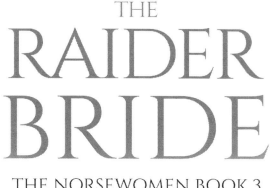

THE
RAIDER
BRIDE

THE NORSEWOMEN BOOK 3

JOHANNA WITTENBERG

For my father, who always said I knew what I was doing.

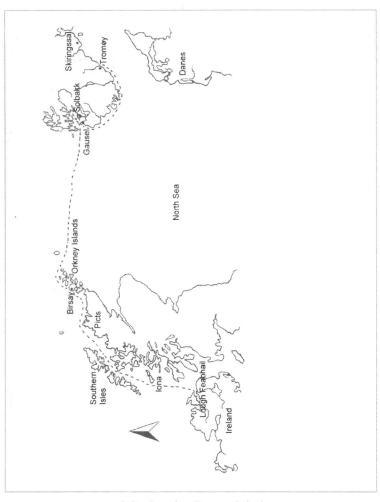

Sailing Route from Tromøy to Ireland

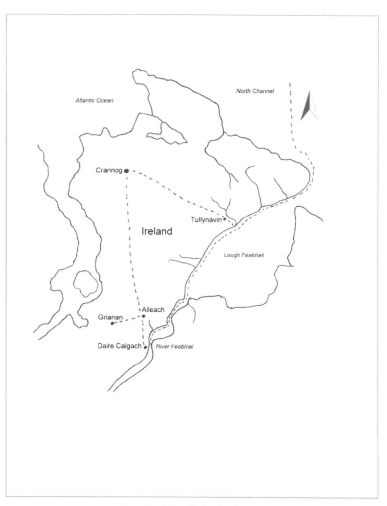

Travels in Ireland by land and water.

able to row either. There was not much use on Tromøy for a cripple.

Ulf was grateful that his own injuries allowed him to function. His legs had been permanently maimed, preventing him from marching any distance or running, but with his massive upper body strength, Ulf could still hold his own in a shield wall and pull an oar with the best of them. Conversely, Behrt had been wounded in the back and the stomach, damaging muscles needed to wield a sword or row a ship. And being a Christian, he couldn't very well become a skáld, or a sorcerer. Those were about the only occupations open to a lame man in the Norse world.

Ulf hoped Behrt would regain his strength with time.

RAGNHILD ENTERED THE DIM HALL, lit only by shafts of daylight from the smoke hole and gable ends and the sullen embers of the longfire. The cavernous room was empty at this time of day, when everyone was out of doors making the most of the early summer weather.

She sat down on the bench and took up her sword, Lady's Servant. She pulled a whetstone from the pouch that hung from her belt and ran the stone across the blade. It was a pointless exercise, for Ulf had forged Lady's Servant from wootz steel, a metal that held an edge like no other. Still, the long, smooth strokes soothed Ragnhild into a mindless trance.

The creak of the outer door jolted her from the reverie. Midday light invaded the hall as Einar burst in. The warrior was out of breath from running.

"It's your brother," he wheezed.

Ragnhild put the whetstone aside and rose, gripping her sword. "Which one?"

"*Wave Rider*," Einar gasped.

"Orlyg." Ragnhild relaxed. "Only one ship?"

Einar nodded, still catching his breath.

"Not an attack, then." Even so, Ragnhild strapped on her sword and picked up her shield.

She followed Einar out of the dim warmth of the hall into the chill wind where Åsa and her household guard were assembling in the yard.

"Einar tells me the ship is your brother's," Åsa said, the question in her voice.

"Orlyg is my younger brother," Ragnhild said. "He wasn't part of my father's attack last year."

"I can't imagine Solvi sending a friendly envoy," said Åsa.

Ragnhild smirked. "Not after we trounced him and he fled home to lick his wounds."

"Or after you raided his hoard."

Ragnhild smiled at the memory of stealing her father's treasure for Åsa. Solvi had sent her elder brother, Harald, to get it back, but Åsa had beaten him, too, and sent him home.

So why was Orlyg here now?

Clouds scurried across the sky, and a spate of rain swatted her in the face. Ragnhild blinked the water out of her eyes as they set off down the trail.

Wave Rider's familiar outline neared the beach. Orlyg's longship carried thirty-five men, enough for raiding a small settlement, but not enough to threaten Tromøy's one hundred well-trained warriors. The dragon figurehead was missing from the prow, sign of peaceful intent.

At a shout, the sail came rattling down. The sailors gathered its folds and lashed it to the yard while rowers ran out their oars and dug blades into the surge.

As they drew close Ragnhild made out her brother at the helm, the wind ruffling his coppery hair as he squinted up at the telltale on the mast, judging the angle of the wind for landing.

She waited just above the tideline. As the keel grounded on

the gravel beach, her gaze met her brother's, and she felt her face twitch into an involuntary smile matching the one that spread across Orlyg's face. An image of him grinning down at her from a tree flashed through her mind. The sudden warmth of the distant memory took her breath away. She had missed him more than she'd realized.

"Welcome, brother." She gripped the prow to steady it as the crew splashed over the side, then stepped away while the warriors heaved the boat up on the beach. Orlyg leaped off the bow and landed at her side, gravel crunching under his boots.

"I am glad to see you, sister!"

Ragnhild lifted her chin to be sure her brother noted the tattoos she'd received on her neck over the winter—the marks of a battle commander. Orlyg's gaze fastened on them and his eyebrows raised in appreciation. Satisfied, Ragnhild turned to Åsa, who waited at the head of her household guards. Tromøy's hird had grown over the winter months. News of Åsa's triumphs over the Danes and Ragnhild's father had spread and attracted warriors, as had rumors of her newfound wealth.

"Åsa Queen, I would like to present my brother, Orlyg, younger son of King Solvi."

Orlyg swept into a low bow. "Greetings, Lady. I come in peace."

Åsa said, "Welcome, Lord Orlyg. You and your men are welcome on my island. You must be weary after your journey. Come to the hall, refresh yourselves."

She started up the trail, her household guard falling in around her. Orlyg shot a glance at Einar, Thorgeir, and Svein, the three húskarlar who had been Solvi's men before swearing to Åsa. Ragnhild tensed. Their faces remained neutral, but hands strayed to sword hilts.

The party climbed the trail to Tromøy's hall. Åsa ushered her guests through the massive oaken doors, intricately carved with entwined beasts picked out in vivid red and blue paint. The workmanship was every bit the equal of Solvi's hall. Ragnhild glanced at her brother to see if he was impressed. His gaze flicked over the carvings, then up to the high roof as he stepped into the entryway.

Inside the great hall, they all stood blinking in the pine-scented gloom. Servants had stirred up the longfire and lit the whale oil lamps that hung from the beams. Åsa commenced the traditional greeting, conducting Orlyg to the guest of honor's place at the far end of the hall. Then she mounted the platform to her high seat. The massive chair was supported with pillars carved with scenes from legend, picked out in vivid paint. In the flickering firelight Odin seemed to cast his spear while his ravens took wing.

The warriors welcomed Orlyg's men among them on the deep benches that ran the length of hall on both sides of the long-fire. Ragnhild made sure her brother was watching when she took her place at the head of her shield-maidens. He commanded a force, and so did she.

Servants carried in basins of warm water, aromatic with herbs, and clean towels. When all had washed, a senior apprentice to the sorceress Heid entered with the silver-chased drinking horn brimming with ale. She served Åsa first, then Orlyg. Ragnhild could barely contain her impatience as the apprentice carried the horn around the longfire.

Once all had drunk the welcome ale, húskarlar and visitors alike settled back expectantly.

"Tell me, Lord Orlyg, what brings you to my shores?" Åsa asked her guest.

Orlyg took a deep breath and turned to Ragnhild. "I have news for my sister. There is no easy way to say this. Father is dead."

The news hit Ragnhild like a fire arrow, searing into her chest. She felt the blood drain from her cheeks.

Why do I care? I owe him nothing. "How?"

"Raiding in Ireland. He was killed by King Murchad." The name sent another shock through Ragnhild. Murchad was the Irish king to whom her father had promised her in marriage, for a treasure in silver.

Like a slave. That's all I was to him, something to sell. Well, I won my freedom.

She realized Orlyg was still speaking to her. "Father sought to take advantage of the disputed kingship in Ireland and start raiding again. But he lost his luck, and Murchad defeated him."

What Orlyg did not say was that Solvi had lost his luck when Åsa had beaten him in battle the year before and Ragnhild had stolen his hoard.

"The Irish ambushed him, and half his crew was slaughtered. Father escaped with his ship and a handful of men, but he died of his wounds on the voyage home. We buried him in the ancestral mound, and Harald stands for king."

Her brother's words kindled a flame in Ragnhild. Now she blurted the words that burned within her. "I will return with you to claim Gausel." Her inheritance. Gausel was a small steading, but it held a strategic position to the seaways, and all the fertile lands of the Jaeren lay under its jurisdiction.

Orlyg dropped his gaze to the table, his ears red at the tips. "Harald believes you took your inheritance when you raided father's hoard. He intends to keep Gausel."

Fury seared Ragnhild's chest, incinerating the shock of her father's death. Silver was one thing, but this was land. Her land. Her brother had no right to it.

"Gausel is odal land," she said. "Mother left it to me. It's mine by right of inheritance. Harald cannot take it."

"He thinks he can," said Orlyg.

Blood thundered in Ragnhild's ears. "I'll fight him for it."

"Ragnhild, you must listen to reason," Orlyg protested. "Harald is not yet king, but he controls the land, and the warriors follow him."

Harald was clever to send this news with Orlyg, the brother closest to her in age. Ragnhild had spent many hours beside him, fishing, training at arms, storytelling, learning the runes. There was a time when they had known each other's innermost hopes. And Harald counted on that.

She shook off those thoughts. "I'm coming with you to claim what's mine."

Orlyg met her gaze. "Harald sails to war, to take revenge on King Murchad."

Of course, Harald could not claim the kingship without avenging Father's death.

Vengeance for a father she'd hated, against a man she'd never met.

But this Irish king had tried to buy her like a thrall, like a peace-cow. It was an insult that humiliated her, made her look weak. If she proved herself in battle against Murchad, Harald could not withhold her land.

"Nevertheless, brother, I'm coming."

Orlyg raised his brows and crossed his arms over his chest. "Harald will not welcome you."

"He can't stop me," she said flatly. "And neither can you."

There was only one who could stop her—the queen who had her oath. Ragnhild looked to Åsa, who said gravely, "I of all people understand vengeance for a father. This is your time. Go, show the world your fierce heart. Your fame will spread far and wide."

Fame. What every warrior needed to open doors in life and to live on after death. Ragnhild had gained a reputation, but a fledgling one. She had bested her father, but he had been an old man. She'd fought the Danes, but only as one of many warriors alongside Åsa. Now she led a hird of shield-maidens who were skilled fighters, but they still had much to prove.

If she sailed with her brothers and took vengeance on the Irish king, her reputation would be made. If she killed her father's slayer, she would be greater than her father. No matter whether she survived the battle, she would live forever in the songs of skálds.

The hunger for it gnawed in her chest.

"It would reflect well on me," Åsa added, "to have you as one of my leaders." She looked at Einar, Svein, and Thorgeir thoughtfully. "The Lady Ragnhild will need experienced warriors to crew her ship. Do you wish to sail with her?"

Ragnhild saw her own desire reflected in their faces.

Orlyg leaned back, narrowing his eyes. "Harald will not welcome traitors."

Åsa ignored him. "Go with Ragnhild," she said to the three warriors. "I expect you to bring her back to me in one piece. Olvir and Jarl Borg will remain here to lead my húskarlar."

"Thank you, Lady," said Einar, casting a defiant gaze at Orlyg.

"I sail with Ragnhild." Heads turned to look at Behrt. The Christian warrior had risen to his feet, and now he met Ragnhild's eye with a resolute expression.

"You can't." Would she never be rid of this man? "You're not fit to make the journey."

Behrt said, "Nevertheless, I sail with you."

Ragnhild turned to Åsa. "You can't allow it."

Åsa regarded Behrt. "You have healed over the winter, but she's right, you are not yet strong enough to make such an arduous voyage."

He lifted his chin. "My queen, my life is my own to do with as I see fit. The Lady Ragnhild spent the winter caring for me, and now I wish to repay the debt. Though not as strong as I was, I can still be of much use on this voyage. I have lived in Ireland and fought beside the Irish. I know their speech and their ways. I know how they make war."

Ragnhild held her tongue, as did everyone in the hall, rather than say what they were all thinking—that a man as crippled as Behrt would be a liability to the entire crew. He walked with difficulty and certainly couldn't pull an oar. It was selfish of him to insist on coming. The others may well have to risk their lives for his.

But nobody said a word. Not a soul in Tromøy's great hall would impugn the courage of the man who had all but given his life to save Ragnhild.

Least of all Ragnhild herself.

"Very well," said Åsa. "You may go."

BEHRT HID his excitement beneath a stone face, but it roiled inside him like surge in a storm.

Ireland.

The very mention of it sent his heart pounding. He hadn't realized how he missed the country, the people and their ways. He longed for their lilting, gentle speech and spritely music, the green land and mild climate, the softness of the air.

He'd never belonged here, though this was the land of his birth. For better or worse, he was an Irishman and a Christian.

Now he sailed with their enemies, to make war on the people he loved—the people who'd cast him out.

What did he hope to accomplish? Could he find a way to protect them from the Norse? He laughed at the idea. He could barely lift his sword. It was more likely he'd stand by and watch the Norse slaughter them.

But he couldn't stay behind. The thought of seeing Ireland again bloomed in his heart, leaving room for nothing else.

And her. He'd be with Ragnhild.

The country of his heart didn't want him, nor the woman. But he couldn't bear to be parted from either of them.

CHAPTER 2

The next day, while Orlyg and his men rested in the guest house, Ragnhild led her crew in outfitting *Raider Bride*. Solvi had it built as her bridal ship, to deliver Ragnhild to her Irish husband. But Ragnhild had seized the vessel and given it a new name.

She smiled grimly. *I will come to you now, husband, and you will wish you'd never met me.*

Her hand-picked crew consisted of eighteen men-at-arms and an equal number of women warriors. Thirty of them were needed to row the ship, plus one helmsman. Ragnhild, Einar, Svein, and Thorgeir were all competent to man the steering oar. The remaining crew would take turns relieving the rowers when needed and tending to other chores aboard ship, such as serving out food, making repairs, and the endless bailing required on a wooden vessel. It remained to be seen what Behrt could do.

Ragnhild looked on the shield-maidens with pride. They were no strangers to hard work, tough as the men and after a year of hard training, equally skilled with weapons. Foremost among them was Unn, a farm girl from the hinterlands. She and her five sisters had joined Åsa's hird at the assembly the year before. Unn was once the second eldest of the sisters, until the oldest, Helga, had been killed in battle against the Danes.

Ragnhild joined Einar, Thorgeir, and Svein as they carefully wrapped their chain-mail brynja in oiled sheepskin and stowed them in their sea chests with their swords and helmets. The rest of the crew packed what they had. Most of them had come fresh off the farm without gear, and Åsa had provided each of them with a helmet, shield, and weapons of the highest quality—swords, spears, and battle-axes. Some had been taken from the vanquished Danes while others were forged in Ulf's workshop. The newest swords were made of precious wootz steel, and bore the inscription "+Ulfbehr+t", named for Tromøy's smith and for Behrt. Behrt had insisted on inscribing the Christ rune on the blades to give protection in battle.

Ragnhild looked up as Behrt emerged from the smithy, trundling his sea chest on a hand cart. From his belt hung a new sword of wootz steel. He'd stow it in his sea chest for the voyage, but no doubt he wanted to show it off. Ragnhild shook her head. Light as it was, could he even wield it?

She gathered with Tromøy's folk on the shore, where the völva Heid and her acolytes sacrificed a goat to bring favor from the gods. Ragnhild joined her crew in the chant as the sorceress anointed the voyagers with sacrificial blood. Heid sprinkled the remaining blood on the prow of each longship.

They loaded the goat's carcass in a cart and hauled it up the trail to the yard, where Toki and his men had kindled the cooking fire. The men butchered the goat and set the meat to simmer in a huge cauldron hung on a tripod over the fire. Then Toki broke out a barrel of mead and another of ale and everyone gathered around the fire to drink while the meat cooked.

Tromøy's folk feasted through the long summer evening. After the meal was eaten, Ragnhild's crew fletched arrows and sharpened blades as they chattered in anticipation of the adventure before them. Most of them were farmers who had never been out of the district, much less on a sea voyage. They would be making a week's voyage around the southern cape to the western side of the mountains to join Harald at Solbakk in Rogaland. From there, Ireland lay far south across the sea. It was a land famed for its beauty and riches. To make such a journey and do battle with an Irish king were the deeds skálds sang of.

"Tell us about Ireland, Behrt," Åsa said.

Behrt's eyes took on a dreamy glaze. "It is a beautiful country, an emerald set on a silken sea."

He must be longing to see the land that was home for most of his life, Ragnhild thought. She hadn't considered it quite that way before. She'd assumed that he wanted to come along to be near her. This trip had been her way to cut ties with Behrt, and now she feared she'd never be rid of him. Still, he was the only one who knew the language, the customs, and the land.

"You were a warrior there," Unn prompted.

The dream-mist cleared from Behrt's eyes. "Yes, I was a slave until I was twelve. Then my master put a sword in my hand and trained me in the ways of the Irish warriors."

"How do they fight?" said Åsa.

"Like cowards," Orlyg blurted.

"They were brave enough to best your father," Behrt countered.

Orlyg's face turned red, but he clamped his jaw shut.

"The Irish are fierce warriors, but they fight differently than the Norse," Behrt said. "They know their terrain and are masters of woodland fighting. They hide in the forests and marshes and attack without warning, then run away—like cowards. But cowards they are not. They are cunning and dangerous. This is something I don't think your elder brother takes into account. To pursue them as they retreat is often a mistake, for they are luring you into a trap where you will find your warriors surrounded."

This statement was met with a long silence as Orlyg glowered. No doubt this was how Solvi met his death.

"They follow the White Christ, and don't believe in our gods," said Ragnhild, to break the tension.

Behrt scowled. "Don't call Him that." The Norse byname for Christ was no compliment. Calling someone "white" was tantamount to calling them a coward.

But Ragnhild was not finished teasing Behrt. "Your god must be lonely. Don't the Irish get bored with one measly deity?"

"God is a Trinity—the Father, Son, and Holy Ghost."

"Your god is a draugr?" Ragnhild referred to the walking dead so feared in Norse folktales.

"No, that's not what I meant! More like a hugr."

"Oh, I see, like a soul that can leave the body and travel on its own, or inhabit the body of an animal," said Åsa, who had much experience with such things.

Behrt shook his head. "That's not exactly right either. It's a mystery we're not meant to fully understand. But the Irish also have many saints."

"What are saints?" asked Unn.

"They are holy people who bless us and perform miracles, even after they die."

Ragnhild's interest perked up at this information. "Like the dís and the álfir in the mound."

Behrt cleared his throat uncomfortably. "Not exactly... The saints are pure of heart and soul, and very devout. They suffer for their holiness."

"Like Odin when he hung from the world-tree for nine nights, to gain the secrets of the runes," Unn chimed in.

"Umm, no," said Behrt. "The saints undergo their ordeals out of devotion to God. But they have powers to equal your gods. For instance, the blessed Colm Cille...he could control the weather. And Saint Patrick, who bested the druid sorcerers with his magic..."

"They're all men!" said Ragnhild, slouching over her ale. "Aren't there any women saints?"

"Yes, of course." Behrt brightened. "Saint Brigid was a mighty warrior for Christ."

Ragnhild sat up. "She sounds interesting."

"Even though she was a woman, Saint Brigid was accorded the same status as Saint Patrick and Saint Colm Cille, though some say it was by accident. She led the virgins of Ireland and performed many miracles."

"What kind of miracles?" asked Unn.

"Well…as a child she gave away all the butter her mother had made to the poor."

"I don't see how that's a miracle," Ragnhild scoffed. "Any fool could do that."

"The miracle was that to keep her from being punished, God replenished the butter she'd given away."

"She sounds very lucky."

"She was favored by God." Behrt warmed to his tale. "She was raised by a druid—an Irish sorcerer—but from birth she was so pure she couldn't eat the druid's profane food. She just vomited it up. They had to bring in a white cow with red ears and twelve virgins to milk it. That's the only nourishment she could take."

Ragnhild snorted. "She sounds like more of a weakling than your White Christ. What else did she do?"

"Well, she gave her father's sword away when someone asked her for it."

Ragnhild snorted again. This time the ale came through her nose.

Fighting these Irish was going to be like picking berries.

IN THE MORNING, Ragnhild joined *Raider Bride's* crew as they geared up in padded battle-jackets made of layers of varnished linen and racked their round wooden shields on the rail. On board they carried an awning that could be set up on the ship or pitched as a tent on shore. Each crewmember had a sea chest and a sheepskin sleeping bag called a hudfat. Åsa had provisioned them with dried meat and fish, root vegetables, a lidded bucket of barley for porridge, and a barrel of freshly brewed ale.

When all was ready, Ragnhild looked to Åsa. She was keen to go, but parting from her queen made her stomach queasy. Ragnhild had become a part of Tromøy, and it was her home now as her father's kingdom had never been.

She knelt before Åsa, her nose stinging with unshed tears. "Lady, I thank you for giving me leave to go, and for your generosity."

"Bring me silver," Åsa said lightly, her own nose a suspicious shade of red.

Ragnhild rose and strode to her ship. She put her shoulder to the gunnel and heaved along with her crew. *Raider Bride* grated across the gravel beach and slid into the water. The karvi bobbed up as the waves met the keel. Ragnhild vaulted over the side and took her place at the helm. Her crew clambered aboard, seated themselves on their sea chests, and fitted the oars. Ragnhild watched Behrt struggle over the sheer strake, stifling the urge to help. It would only humiliate him.

When at last all were aboard and the rowers had taken up their oars, she called out the strokes. As *Raider Bride* cut through the water, she aimed the bow at *Wave Rider's* stern and followed her brother out of Tromøy's harbor. As they emerged from the bay's shelter, Ragnhild held her face to the wind and let the chill caress whip her spirits to life.

"Raise sail!" she cried. The rowers shipped their oars and scurried to throw off the ties that bound the sail to the yard. "Heave!"

The crew hauled on the walrus-hide halyard, and the wood parrel dragged the massive yard up the mast. Behrt took his place in line and pulled with the rest. The heavy sail spilled free. The wind caught the fabric and the sail shuddered like the wings of a gull. *Raider Bride* came alive, surging into the choppy seas.

Ragnhild heaved the steering oar over, bringing the ship on a southwesterly course. The crew sheeted the big sail home, and *Raider Bride* quivered like a bowstring drawn taut. She dug her bow into the waves and forged ahead.

The sun glimmered and the wind held through the long summer day. The two vessels sailed companionably within sight of each other, making good time. Ragnhild took the lead, reveling in the freedom.

Many of her crew were first-timers, and their first taste of choppy seas brought their stomachs to their throats. Ragnhild laughed with the other seasoned sailors while the green ones gave their breakfasts to the sea. "You'll get your sea legs soon enough."

The freshening wind thrummed in the rigging and the waves foamed white at the bow. Thorgeir raised his voice in a sea song and, sickness forgotten, everyone joined in.

As evening closed, Ragnhild led the way into a sheltered cove. They beached their ships and made camp. Excited from their first day at sea, the crew chattered as they feasted on smoked pork and ale Åsa had provided. Ragnhild eyed Behrt, who slumped to the ground and drooped against a log, his face a worrisome shade of white. If this trip killed him, would it be her fault? She watched him manage to gulp down a bit of ale and some food, and the color returned to his face. He even smiled at something Unn said. He'd survive. Ragnhild turned her attention to her brother, who was in the mood to reminisce.

"Do you remember when we tried to sail to the Orkney Islands?" said Orlyg.

Ragnhild smiled. "What were we, ten and twelve? We only made it to the entrance of the bay. I could never forget that!"

"Nor can we," Einar said. "Your father nearly outlawed us for letting you get that far."

"It's a good thing we caught you before you made it outside in that little skiff," Thorgeir said.

"Yes, a good thing for all of us," Ragnhild agreed. The three húskarlar had always been there, watching over her and her brothers as they grew. Keeping them safe. Without them, Solvi's foolhardy children would not have survived to adulthood.

The summer sky was darkening to a deep blue, the stars emerging like gems on a völva's cloak. One by one the crew made their way to their sleeping skins. As Ragnhild crawled into her hudfat, a sense of anticipation came over her that she had not felt in a long time. She was going home.

CHAPTER 3

Southern Coast of Norway

In the morning the crews dropped their casual pace as they raced to strike camp and get underway. The familiar thrill of competition took hold, and Ragnhild drove her crew to be first to launch. Orlyg was of the same mind, and the two ships slid into the water simultaneously. Warriors leaped aboard and ran out the oars, the competitive fever catching the crews as they drove their craft across the glassy water of the bay. Even Behrt moved with alacrity, getting over the gunnels unaided. The night's rest seemed to have done him good.

"Row!" Ragnhild shouted as her crew strove to keep up with Orlyg's ship. Their bows were even as they made the cove's entrance.

The two ships ducked behind the archipelago of skerries and islets that formed an inner passage, sheltered from the dangerous seas off the southern coast.

As the smaller ship, *Raider Bride* had the advantage maneuvering in the narrow, skerry-littered passage. Throughout the morning, Ragnhild maintained her lead, dodging rocks and playing the currents. The crew was silent as they concentrated on keeping their oars from breaking on the skerries.

By midafternoon the islets thinned and they neared the rocky headland of Lindesnes, the southern tip of land. As they came out from the shelter of the last islet, the wind hit them, kicking up choppy seas. It was a good breeze. Ragnhild considered for a moment whether they should portage across the headland. Summer was the only time of year to brave the seas off the southern cape, but even now they could be dangerous in a blow. This wind was right on the edge.

She looked over at *Wave Rider*. Orlyg's crew had taken in their oars and were heading for the mast.

"Ship oars!" Ragnhild cried. "Make sail!"

Both crews raced to unlash their sails and haul the heavy yards up the mast. Orlyg got his sail up and drawing an instant earlier than Ragnhild. *Wave Rider* surged ahead, and Ragnhild shouted at her crew to tweak the sheets, squeezing every bit of speed out of the ship. She couldn't let her brother take the lead now. *Wave Rider* was longer on the waterline than *Raider Bride,* making her brother's ship inherently faster in open water. Once he got ahead of her, she would never catch him.

The wind freshened, coming aft as they rounded the cape, and Ragnhild felt the tiller quiver as *Raider Bride* began to surf. The ship came up on the wave and tried to shake off the steering oar. Ragnhild knew she should take a reef in the sail, but Orlyg wasn't making a move to do so. If she shortened sail now, *Raider Bride* would lose ground to the larger ship, distance they'd never make up. Her gaze flicked to Einar and he nodded. Take the risk. Thorgeir and Svein grinned their agreement. Ragnhild firmed her grip on the tiller and forced herself to relax. Steering was a matter of feeling now, sensing the wind shifts and wave patterns. She had to move with the ship rather than try to control it.

The newer crewmembers clung to the shrouds, shouting with joy as the spray hit them, too inexperienced to realize their danger. Their seasickness seemed to be behind them. Behrt sat with his back against the hull, smiling into the wind. Ragnhild felt a bit of her tension ease.

As they rounded land's end, the ship heeled over, dipping her rail in the water, scooping up spray as *Raider Bride* took the full force of the wind across her beam. Once they were safely past the cape, Ragnhild headed northwest and the wild ride was over. The seas fell in behind, pushing the ship homeward with a soft, steady whoosh. Looking aft, Ragnhild glimpsed *Wave Rider* surging in their wake. Orlyg waved, a huge grin splitting his face.

Halfway up the coast, they put into a sandy cove for the night so they would arrive at Solbakk in daylight. While the crew roistered around the campfire, Ragnhild was more silent than usual. She would be coming home for the first time in a year. The last time, she had been her father's prisoner.

As they launched next morning, Orlyg shouted, "First boat in gets the first horn of ale."

Ragnhild shook off her somber mood and threw herself into the race. Now that they had rounded the southern cape and entered their home waters, she and her brother were evenly matched on local knowledge. To compensate for *Wave Rider's* greater speed, Ragnhild had to employ tactics and hope she could outdo Orlyg with seamanship alone.

They sailed by the familiar stretches of dunes and sandy beaches of the Jaeren coast, territory subject to Gausel, Ragnhild's birthright. Where she could, Ragnhild took advantage of current and wind variation. She gave the helm over to Einar and played the sheets, adjusting the sail to squeeze every last bit of speed out of the ship. Through constant concentration, Ragnhild managed to stay even with her brother.

Around midday a scattering of islands appeared off the coast, signaling home waters. The two ships rounded the headland together, Ragnhild and Orlyg laughing at their hard-won draw. The Boknafjord opened up before them. Prows aligned, they roared past the island where their father's war beacon perched on a cliff like a giant nest.

In the fjord's protected waters, the crews dropped the sails and took up their oars. Ragnhild clung to the prow, straining to catch sight of the settlement. Memories gusted through her, stirring up feelings like ghosts.

She spotted the great hall on the hill. A woman emerged, raising an arm to shade her eyes. For an instant Ragnhild saw her mother waiting for her. But her mother was long dead, and as the ships drew closer the familiarity faded, and the figure resolved into a stranger.

A knot of men waited on the shore. In the late afternoon light, Ragnhild picked out Harald among his húskarlar. Tall and golden-haired, her older brother looked like a man born to be king. Ragnhild fought down uncertainty and the guilt that came with it. She had betrayed her family, but only after they had betrayed her. Her father had drilled into his children that duty to the family came before self, and she had chosen herself over them. A choice she did not regret.

The ship grounded gently on the shore. Her crew splashed over the side and hauled *Raider Bride* up the beach. Ragnhild stepped off the bow and crunched into the gravel of her homeland. Her throat caught as she recognized familiar faces in the crowd. She reminded herself she was no longer the rebellious girl who had run away in the dead of winter. She was a warrior, a shield-maiden, soon to be chieftain of her own land.

Raising her chin, Ragnhild faced her elder brother. His gaze lit on her tattoos, but his face betrayed no reaction.

Up close, Harald looked even more kingly in a fine red wool cloak with a fur collar and tablet-woven trim. A band of silver bound his blond hair. He had filled out—his shoulders broad, his golden beard lush.

She held his gaze without a smile. "Brother."

He returned her nod, as unsmiling as she. "Welcome, sister." He inspected her crew, staring pointedly at Einar, Thorgeir, and Svein, whom his father had named traitors. He opened his mouth as if to speak, but just then, Orlyg came trotting up.

"She almost beat me," he crowed. Harald's glare dissolved and he slung his arm around her shoulders.

"Well done, little sister."

Pride surged in Ragnhild at Harald's praise. Suddenly it was like old times and, side by side, the three siblings led their crews up the trail to the hall.

The woman Ragnhild had mistaken for her mother waited by the door. Harald put his arm around the stranger, who smiled up at him. "Ragnhild, this is my wife, Signy."

Harald, married. Shock coursed through her. She drew a deep breath and returned the smile. Signy was a pretty woman with brown hair and calm gray eyes, plump and a little shorter than Ragnhild. From close up, the resemblance to their mother was less marked, but Signy's every gesture, and the cadence of her speech, summoned memories. Ragnhild wondered if Harald was conscious of the likeness.

"Signy is the daughter of King Orm of Sogn," said Harald proudly.

So. A cousin of their mother's. That explained the haunting similarities. And Signy was an only child. The marriage would likely make Harald King of Sogn one day.

"Welcome, sister." Signy took her arm in a familiar way and Ragnhild felt instantly comforted. "Come into the hall, refresh yourself."

Ragnhild found herself following Signy meekly. *Like a lamb to slaughter.*

Inside the hall, Ragnhild stiffened, bracing for her father's voice to boom his disapproval at her. In the next instant she realized that voice had been stilled forever. Relief flooded her, followed by a sense of loss that hit like a thunderclap, leaving her weak-kneed and hollow.

All through this tide of emotions she bore a stone face, but the skin of it felt brittle as a crust of dried mud, ready to flake away at the smallest disturbance.

Her sister-in-law guided her gently to the guest seat and settled her, while the brothers took their places, Harald on the high seat, Orlyg at the head of the húskarlar. There was a tense moment as Einar, Thorgeir, and Svein faced their former compatriots. But just as things were getting awkward, one of Harald's warriors rose and offered Einar a seat. With a breath of relief, Ragnhild watched her crew find places among Solbakk's hird.

The longfire crackled cleanly, scenting the air with pine. Servants brought basins of warm water and towels and waited while Ragnhild and her crew washed away the salt and grime of the trip.

Signy carried the drinking horn brimming with ale to her husband, and spoke the words mandated by ceremony. Next she served Orlyg, and when he had drunk she approached Ragnhild.

She proffered the horn gravely. "Drink, sister, daughter of Solvi, honored guest."

As if in a dream, Ragnhild accepted the horn and let the welcome ale slide past her lips. It was so peculiar to be served as a guest in her father's hall, where once she had done the serving. She handed the horn back, and her eyes met Signy's, whose smile caught, lifting the cloud of strangeness.

Signy served the other guests. Once the greeting ceremony was complete and cups were filled, Ragnhild waited for her brother to get down to business.

"I am happy you have come to visit us, sister," Harald began, not sounding a bit happy. "I assume Orlyg has told you of our father's death."

Ragnhild speared a morsel of lamb with her knife and ate it, then looked at her brother. "I have come to claim Gausel."

Harald flicked his gaze toward her nervously. She could see the boy peering out of his eyes, though he sat upon the high seat. "Orlyg should have explained that you have already received your inheritance."

Ragnhild tamped down on her resentment. *Focus on what you want from this.* "I took Solvi's hoard in a raid. It's booty, not inheritance. Gausel was Mother's dowry, and rightly mine."

Harald glared at her. "She left it for your dowry. Why don't you find a nice lord to marry? Then we'll talk about it."

The air whooshed, ruffling his hair as Ragnhild's eating knife thwacked into the pillar beside his head. Silence fell over the hall. Harald's nostrils flared, but he did not flinch or even look at the knife as it quivered beside him.

"I think your sister has made her point," said Signy drily.

"I need no man to get my inheritance for me." Ragnhild rose and strode to the high seat. She yanked her knife from the pillar and brandished the blade in Harald's face. "I will fight you for it, brother."

Harald jerked his head away impatiently. "I have no time for such games. I sail within the week to take vengeance on the Irish king."

"And I sail with you," said Ragnhild.

"We have no need of you."

"Nevertheless, I am coming." Their eyes locked as she stood facing him, knife ready.

Signy's voice chimed into the heavy silence. "Let us speak no more of this tonight." She called for mead and signaled Egil, the skáld, who rose and cleared his throat.

Ragnhild turned from her brother and resumed her seat. She

managed to keep a stone face while Egil delivered a lengthy praise poem memorializing Solvi's victories in battle. She noted sourly that no mention was made of his defeat in Tromøy, nor did Egil celebrate any of Ragnhild's triumphs.

That will change soon enough.

Though they glared at each other whenever their eyes met over the longfire, Ragnhild and Harald obeyed their hostess and avoided the subjects of Gausel or the raid. As the evening wore on, the celebrants began to slump a little in their seats. Behrt once again looked pale and drawn. Ragnhild was glad that Einar and Thorgeir flanked him. They'd look after the Christian.

Signy rose, signaling the women. Ragnhild stood and her shield-maidens got to their feet. They followed Signy across the moonlit yard to the women's bower, a building nearly as large as the great hall. Servants waited at the door.

Solbakk's women made room for Ragnhild's shield-maidens on the fur-covered benches surrounding the central longfire. The fire burned dry and clean, and the room filled with friendly chatter as the women settled in for the night.

Signy paused at the door to the queen's bedchamber—the room Ragnhild had once shared with her mother. The room that had been Ragnhild's own after her mother's death. Her feet seemed stuck to the packed-earth floor.

Then Signy smiled and opened the door. "Please, sister, come in."

The awkward moment passed and Ragnhild followed Signy into the chamber.

Katla, her old fóstra, greeted her. "My lamb, I am so glad to see you!" the aging woman exclaimed, folding Ragnhild in her arms. The familiar scent of thyme filled her nose and suddenly she wanted to weep.

"I am glad to see you, too," she said, giving Katla's frail shoulders a careful hug.

She let her nurse fuss over her, standing patiently while the old woman helped her out of battle jacket and breeks and drew a clean linen shift over her head. She sat on the stool by the fire while Katla unplaited her salt-stiff braid and combed it soft and shining. When all was done she embraced her nurse and climbed into the big feather bed beside Signy, who had undressed herself.

"How does it feel to be home?" Signy asked.

Ragnhild snorted. "This is my home no longer."

Signy raised herself up on one elbow and gazed into Ragnhild's eyes. "This will always be your home."

"Gausel is my home now. I have come to claim it."

"Be patient with Harald. He will come around in time." It sounded almost as if Signy was on her side.

"Harald does not want me to come to Ireland."

"Harald still underestimates you," said Signy. "It is an older brother's failing. He's decided to leave Orlyg here, he says to take charge in his absence. Yet I have no need for a half-grown boy to look after things. In truth it is for Orlyg's safety that he leaves him behind, and the same applies to you."

Ragnhild punched her pillow. "I will prove myself to Harald, and then he cannot refuse me Gausel."

Signy looked at her sadly. "Take care that you survive, sister. In the end that's all that matters."

"How can you say that? It's better to die with honor and go to Freyja's hall than to languish in Hel's cold realm."

"That is what the warriors believe," said Signy carefully.

"And you do not?"

"I do not."

"What then?"

Signy drew a silver cross from beneath her shift.

Ragnhild jolted upright. "Another Christian!" She stared at the glittering cross.

"It's a religion of love and compassion."

"For women, it's a religion of enslavement." Ragnhild had been raised on stories of the Franks and how they forced their brutal laws on the Saxons, stripping the women of their rights to divorce and property, rendering them the chattel of fathers and husbands.

Signy's face darkened. "I'm no slave. I'm soon to be a queen. I've given up none of my rights."

The proud words gave Ragnhild pause. "How did you come to worship the White Christ?"

"My father had an Irish slave who was a Christian monk." Signy's gaze softened as she seemed to look far away. "Brother Elagh was my tutor, and he showed me the beauty of Christianity, while he lived. When my father found out that he had converted me, he had Brother Elagh killed. He died a martyr's death." Signy kissed the cross. "I will never forget him."

"But Harald…"

"My husband has yet to embrace the true faith."

"Well, thank Thor for that! I'm surprised he allows you to practice the religion."

"Your brother cannot tell me what God to worship." Signy's gray eyes flashed in the firelight.

This brought Ragnhild up short. Perhaps there was more grit to her sister-in-law than she thought.

Signy patted the pillow beside her invitingly. "Come, I'm not sacrificing pagans tonight."

Ragnhild realized she was shivering. She burrowed under the eiderdown comforter next to her warm Christian sister-in-law.

CHAPTER 4

Solbakk

Ragnhild woke alone in the big feather bed. Signy was nowhere to be seen. Ragnhild wondered how late it was. She hurried out of bed and into Katla's arms.

"What time of day is it? Where is everyone?"

"Lady Signy bade me let you sleep," said Katla. "I will help you dress and you can join the others in the hall for breakfast."

Katla had laid out a clean linen shift and an overdress of soft blue wool that looked familiar, but Ragnhild could not place it. Certainly she had not brought any lady's clothes, but only a second set of woolen breeks and tunic, with linen undershirts.

"It was your mother's," said Katla, gesturing at the dress. "It should be a good fit."

Ragnhild noted her sea chest had been carried up and placed in the corner of the room. Inside should be her chain-mail brynja, helmet, axe, and long sword. The salt-stained leather battle-jacket she had worn throughout the voyage hung from a peg on the wall beside her baldric and short sword. With a flare of guilt, she remembered the bridal linens that Katla had so proudly presented her with, to take to her new home in Ireland. The old nurse must have spent months embroidering the dainty garments.

"I am sorry I didn't bring the beautiful things you made for me," she said. "I didn't want to ruin them. They are safe on Tromøy." She did not add that they now lay moldering in a trunk in Tromøy's bower, untouched.

Katla nodded, seemingly satisfied with Ragnhild's lame explanation. "I don't expect you will have many chances to wear them on this trip." She did not mention that they had been intended for Ragnhild's wedding to the same Irish king they now set out to kill.

Ragnhild stood patiently as Katla pulled the linen shift over her head, followed by the woolen jumper. The fóstra clasped the jumper's straps with two domed oval silver brooches, cast in an intricately interlaced mold. Between the brooches hung a triple strand of beads, fine colored glass, amber, and silver. A memory flashed through Ragnhild's mind of her mother wearing them.

Feeling dizzy to be dressed in her mother's clothes, she sat to pull on soft leather boots and draw the thick woolen shawl over her shoulders, then rose and walked out the door Katla held open for her.

Outside the bower it was bright daylight. From inside the great hall came the sound of laughter and the clatter of eating knives.

She entered and took her place on the guest seat, across the longfire from her brothers and sister-in- law.

Signy smiled at her. "I hope you rested well, sister," she said.

"Indeed, I did. You should have wakened me."

"We thought you needed extra sleep after your long journey."

No one mentioned that Orlyg had made the same journey, or

for that matter Ragnhild's crew, who were well into their breakfasts.

These thoughts were interrupted when a servant set a steaming bowl of barley porridge and a cup of small beer on the trestle before Ragnhild. Although she had eaten well the night before, the aroma of porridge made her stomach growl. She picked up her spoon and attacked her breakfast. When the last of the porridge was gone, she leaned back in her seat to sip her beer. She did not want to bring up the subject of Gausel now. Best wait until she had proven herself on this Irish venture. Harald would have a hard time refusing her after that.

"When do we leave?" she asked, looking at Harald over the rim of her cup.

"*I* depart in two days' time."

Well, you can't stop me from following, brother.

"What do you know of this king?" she asked. "What is your plan of attack?"

"Father was ambushed as soon as he landed. The Irish were ready for him and we think they had been forewarned of his arrival, possibly by a lookout on one of the headlands. We must be better prepared than Father was." Harald relaxed as he expounded on his strategy. "We have allies in the Orkney Islands. We will stop there on our way to gather information and plan our attack."

Ragnhild marked how "I" had changed to "we." She said no more, letting the delicate truce gain traction.

After breakfast she called her crew together. They assembled on the beach beside *Raider Bride*.

"You know the way to Ireland, in case he manages to leave us behind," she said to Einar.

The warrior looked at Thorgeir and Svein. "We have made the voyage several times with your father, although it was years ago. The first leg of the journey is easy, for the Orkneys lie due west of here. We can find our way." Thorgeir and Svein nodded.

"I know the way, and I've made the passage here just over a year ago," said Behrt. "I sailed from the west coast of Ireland, through the Southern Islands and along the coast of Alba, then through the Orkneys. We landed at Avaldsnes, just to the north of here."

"And you have fought with these Irish," Ragnhild said. "You speak their language and know their ways."

Behrt nodded. "That's something you have not shared with your elder brother."

Ragnhild smiled. "That gives us an advantage. And knowing Harald, we may need it."

A COLD DRAFT woke Ragnhild as Signy slid out of bed. Fighting the urge to snuggle back under the down comforter, she forced her eyes open and watched her sister-in-law dress in the dim light that filtered through the gable end. When Signy slipped out the door, Ragnhild rose, shivering, and fumbled for her clothes in the chest at the foot of the bed. She could tell by their clean scent that Katla had washed them. She drew on tunic and breeks, jammed her feet into her soft leather boots and hurried after Signy.

In the bower the women still slept on their benches. She quietly made her way to the entry, opened the door, and slipped out.

Blinking in the early sunlight, she searched for Signy, but there was no sign of her. Ragnhild started toward the hall when the sound of retching drew her to the back of the bower. Signy crouched in the bushes, vomiting. She looked up as Ragnhild approached.

"Are you all right?"

Signy nodded, wiping her mouth. "It's normal," she croaked.

It took Ragnhild a moment to understand. "Oh! Congratulations!"

"Thanks."

"Does Harald know?"

"Yes, but we are not going to announce it until we are sure it's taken."

Ragnhild understood. Even royal parents-to-be didn't get their hopes up until after the birth. Babies slipped away too easily in the first months of pregnancy. Even after a successful birth, infants were not given a name or presented to their fathers until they had survived nine days outside the womb.

Ragnhild took Signy's hand and helped her to her feet. "I wish you all the best. I won't say anything."

"Thank you, sister. I think I can face up to breakfast now. Shall we go in?"

AFTER A BREAKFAST of skyr topped with a scattering of wild berries, Ragnhild joined the others on the beach, where the cauldron of pine tar sent pungent steam into the air. Harald's splendid ship, *Battle Swan*, lay alongside *Raider Bride*, its prow overhanging hers by an arm span. But *Raider Bride* was sleeker, with a finer entry that would cut into the seas.

They worked in the brisk, sunlit air, going over the ships in preparation for the three-day passage across the open sea to the Orkney Islands. Harald and Einar recaulked the hulls, driving fresh wool into the seams between the lapped oak strakes, and sealing them with pine tar. The women inspected the sails and reinforced tears and thin spots. Ragnhild and Behrt joined those examining the ropes of hemp and seal hide, relaying worn places if the rope could be salvaged or replacing them altogether if they were too far gone.

Ragnhild worked in a simmer of anticipation. Though she had

been on the sea all of her life, she had never spent a night out of sight of land. The thought of endless horizons drove a spear point of excitement and fear into her heart.

The day passed in a blur of work, and then Ragnhild trooped up to the hall with her shipmates for the farewell feast. Settled amid the rowdy group, she relished her ale and mutton while excited chatter rose into the high rafters of the hall. Harald was in a rare mood, passing the ale horn again and again. He spoke of the voyage through the northern and southern isles, of Ireland and its riches, igniting her imagination. When she finally staggered off to bed, ale and exhaustion submerged her instantly in sleep.

IT SEEMED she had just closed her eyes when Signy shook her awake.

"Hurry, sister. Breakfast is being served."

Ragnhild's heart thudded in her chest as she scrambled out of bed. Her head was fuzzy as if it had been packed with wool, and her tongue was dry as an old shoe. Wishing she hadn't drunk quite so much, she yanked on her clothes and boots, then hefted her sea chest and lugged it out to the yard. Fortunately the cart still waited there, and she shoved her chest atop the others.

The hall was empty when she got there, so she bolted her porridge and hurried to the beach.

Harald ignored her as she joined her crew readying *Raider Bride*. Orlyg was assisting them, and Ragnhild thought he looked a little forlorn at being left behind. Signy arrived, driving the horse-drawn cart loaded with sea chests and barrels of flatbread, dried fish, venison, cabbages, and ale for the journey.

She jumped down from the cart and hugged Ragnhild. "God go with you, sister."

Tears prickled at her eyes and Ragnhild swallowed hard as she returned the hug. "When I return, I will bring gifts for your child."

They lined up on either side of their ships, loading the stores and sea chests. When the last barrel was aboard, Harald glared at her over *Battle Swan's* gunnels. "Don't expect me to rescue you when you get into trouble."

Ragnhild sent him a wolfish smile. "Don't worry about me, brother."

A ghost of a grin flashed across Harald's face in reply, before he froze it back into a scowl.

"Heave!" he cried, and they dragged their ships to the water. As the keels splashed into the shallows, Ragnhild leaped aboard with her crew and they scrambled for oars, eager to get ahead of the other ship.

Amid cheers and shouts, Ragnhild and her crew jockeyed for the lead through familiar islets and skerries. The state of the tide was ingrained in her like a childhood song. Though the water appeared smooth, beneath the surface snarled riptides and back eddies. Ragnhild knew just where *Raider Bride* could skim over submerged rocks and where they would rip her planks out.

Harald knew them as well as she did, and he gave no quarter as they raced through the turbulent currents. *Battle Swan's* length gave him no advantage in the constricted waterways, but Ragnhild knew she must have a healthy lead before they broke out into open water, when the *Swan's* longer waterline gave Harald the advantage.

The swells were mounting, signaling the proximity of the sea.

"You're getting a little close," Einar warned as Ragnhild scraped by a big skerry. With a crash, *Raider Bride* grounded. The ship stuck fast, quivering, while Harald swept past, his crew jeering.

Face hot with shame, Ragnhild shipped the steering oar. She leaped from the stern onto the rock, slick with kelp.

Einar was already beside her on the skerry. "The tide is

rising," he soothed. "We'll refloat, the question is when." He helped Ragnhild keep a firm grip on the gunnels as Svein and Thorgeir stepped onto the rock. The rough leather soles of their boots gripped the slippery surface. They held the ship as the seas shifted the bow and rippled along the keel to the stern, grating the timbers on the rock. The crew on board steadied themselves on their sea chests, oars raised clear of the skerry.

Ragnhild focused on holding *Raider Bride's* skittish hull so she wouldn't have to watch Harald's stern dwindle in the distance. Time enough to gauge his lead when they were afloat. She fought back tears as the swells ground the ship into the rock over and over. How much could *Raider Bride* withstand? She was a fool.

"Soon," said Einar. "Keep a sharp eye on the tide."

Ragnhild's eyes widened at the smooth-backed swell that rippled toward them.

"This is it."

They clung to the gunnels as the swell lifted the hull. Ragnhild's feet lost traction as she shoved off, praying it had been enough. She tumbled into the bottom of the boat. Einar and the others dove in after her while the boat rose and then, sickeningly, dropped. The stern cracked against the rock, making Ragnhild wince.

"Row!" she shouted, scrambling up to reseat the steering oar. The oars bit into the waves and the boat shot forward.

"We need to inspect the hull," Einar said.

"We'll never catch Harald," she muttered.

"Einar's right. We can't make the crossing without checking the hull," said Thorgeir. "We'll catch up to him in Orkney."

"What if he leaves without us?"

Einar shrugged. "If the ship is sound, we won't lose that much time. If it's not, then it will be as the gods decide."

They put ashore in the lee of an islet. Ragnhild held her breath as they examined the ragged-looking keel, but there were no structural cracks. While Einar and Thorgeir saw to the repairs and planed the oak smooth, Ragnhild sat alone on the bow, still shaken by the near disaster.

Unn approached her, bearing smoked fish, flatbread, and two cups of ale.

"You need to eat, Lady," she said.

Ragnhild accepted the cup. She took the bread but could not bring it to her mouth.

"I risked my ship—and my crew—for what?" she blurted. "A foolish race. Perhaps I am not ready to be a leader."

Unn grinned over her cup. "It was fun."

"It's my duty to protect my crew."

Now Unn chuckled. "Lady, if we wanted to be safe, we'd have stayed at home with Queen Åsa. We're warriors, not farmers. We follow you for adventure, for booty, for glory. We follow you because we know you'll lead us into danger."

Ragnhild stared at the shield-maiden.

"We are just like you, but you're more daring than the rest of us. That's why we follow you."

Thorgeir made his way to the bow. "I'd say she'll float."

Unn rose. "Now, we need to catch your brother."

CHAPTER 5

R aider Bride got underway in the midafternoon. The waves
developed sharp edges as they emerged from protected
waters and the last of the islands dwindled in the distance. They
hauled up the sails in the freshening breeze. Standing in the
center of the ship, Einar stretched his arm out toward the sun
and made a fist. He sighted down his arm and measured the
height of the sun. "It's nearly Eykt," he said, referring to the hour
that was exactly midafternoon. Then he set a course for the
Orkney Islands.

Ragnhild was relieved that Einar had taken a sighting, though
on this voyage there was little chance of hafvilla—getting lost at
sea. It was easy enough to track the course due west, and if they
missed the Orkneys, they would undoubtedly find the Shetland
Islands to the north.

As *Raider Bride* plunged into the seas, a sense of freedom
welled up within Ragnhild, vast as the crisp blue expanse,
tinged with a delicious edge of fear. Her field of vision
stretched to the horizon in every direction. She was acutely
aware of how thin the overlapping planks were as they flexed in
the seaway, always shipping a little water between the seams,

and how low in the water the gunnels sat as the waves leaped aboard.

A few of the farmhands turned pale as the ship rolled in the swells. Ragnhild watched them vomit over the side with sympathy.

"I am sorry, Lady," Unn croaked, wiping her mouth.

"It's only luck," said Ragnhild. "Some of the mightiest warriors fall to seasickness. It will pass."

As the sky's blue deepened to cobalt, Ragnhild set watches to let those who were not heaving over the side get some sleep. Einar took a bearing on the setting sun, then relieved her on the helm, and she snuggled into her sheepskin. She gazed up at the stars, listening to the hiss and gurgle of water creaming past the hull while *Raider Bride* rose and fell rhythmically in the seas. Sleep came easily, and she woke to relieve the watch, more alive than she had ever felt before.

When dawn broke, the wind was fair, sending *Raider Bride* racing over the waves. The green crewmembers gained their sea legs and their eyes took on a sparkle. They fell into a comfortable rhythm of sleep and work, taking their turns as lookouts, washing down flatbread and dried meat with a cup of ale, burrowing under the furs for a nap in the shelter of the bow. Work was endless, coiling lines, bailing the bilge, trimming the sail to suit the breeze.

Einar, Thorgeir, Svein, and Ragnhild each took a turn on the helm. Svein and Thorgeir taught the crew sea songs while Behrt told them tales of Irish heroes.

"The king we seek vengeance against is of the Ui Neill, descendants of Niall of the Nine Hostages," said Behrt. "Niall was a great king who conquered all the kingdoms of Ireland, Scotland, Francia, and Britain, and took hostages from each of them. They say he gained his kingship by making love to an ugly hag who was really Aine, goddess of Ireland, in disguise."

Ragnhild was fascinated to learn all she could about the man she intended to kill, but the crew's favorite hero was Finn mac Cumhail. "He grew up hidden deep in the forest," said Behrt, "raised by two women, one a druid, the other a huntress. His foster mothers trained him to be expert in their arts so that he could one day avenge his father's murder.

"When Finn could outrun the deer, his foster mothers sent him to a chieftain to learn warfare. To gain his place, he fought all the chieftain's other youths. When he'd beaten them all, he studied with a great poet who lived by a mighty river where he caught the salmon of wisdom. The poet left Finn to watch over the salmon while it cooked, but forbade him to taste the fish."

"This tale is beginning to sound familiar," said Ragnhild. "Does he burn his thumb on the hot broth, and stick it in his mouth to ease the pain?" The Norse knew the tale of Sigurd the dragon slayer, who tasted a dragon's heart under similar circumstances.

"Yes," said Behrt, "but the poet doesn't try to kill Finn like Sigurd's mentor. Instead, he acknowledges that the gods intended Finn to gain the magic of the salmon."

Ragnhild mulled over the Irish tale and the Norse. There was quite a difference between slaying a dragon and catching a fish. Nonetheless, Finn sounded like a formidable warrior. She looked forward to meeting one of his descendants in battle.

AT DAWN on the third day, flocks of puffins and other seabirds appeared. Soon, the rugged cliffs of the Orkneys loomed on the horizon. Ragnhild felt a twinge of disappointment that the passage was over. One day, she would keep going, far beyond the known lands.

Einar guided them in, skirting the crashing surf to make landfall on the leeward side of what proved to be a tidal island, connected to a larger land mass only when the tide was out, exposing a rocky stretch of land. They beached beside *Battle Swan* on a quiet strand by the natural causeway below a rock-walled, turf-roofed longhouse.

Four spearmen waited on shaggy ponies.

"Welcome," one of the sentries called. "Our lord has been waiting for you."

Ragnhild disembarked, and the land heaved beneath her feet as if she were still at sea. She reeled into Einar, who gripped her elbow. The farmhands swayed with her, wide-eyed.

"We've lost our land legs," she reassured them. "It will pass by morning. Just walk with care."

They staggered after the horsemen up the trail to the long-house. The settlement boasted two outbuildings, a scattering of sheep in the pasture, and a field green with barley. Drifting down from the longhouse, the scent of ale and meat cooking foretold a feast already in the making.

A tall gray-beard stood in the doorway, surrounded by more spearmen. "Greetings. I am Ivar, chieftain here," he said. "Your brother is waiting for you."

Harald stepped forward. "It took you long enough, sister," he smirked. Ragnhild's face burned. Before she could answer, Harald turned to their host. "May I present my sister, Ragnhild Solvisdottir."

"Welcome, Lady Ragnhild, come in and take refreshment." Ivar ushered them into the hall where Harald's crew were already drinking ale on benches around the smoky turf longfire.

A woman in her middle years stood inside the door. Her brown hair, threaded with silver strands, was braided and coiled in a complex style. Her gown and shawl were of fine-woven wool, dyed the rich purple of mollusks, embroidered with red dragons in silken thread.

"I am Gudrun." She led them to the guest seats while Ivar settled Harald beside him on the high seat.

Gudrun accepted an ale horn from a servant and served the

latecomers. When Ragnhild's turn came, she drank carefully, then settled back on her bench and watched the room undulate.

When they had drunk, Harald looked at Ivar. "You were telling me of Murchad's fortifications."

"The Cenel nEoghan have an ancient fortress high on the summit of a mountain, commanding a view of the countryside all the way to the sea," said Ivar. "Murchad will know you're coming long before you land. That was likely your father's undoing."

"How can we avoid that problem? It's not as if we can hide our approach."

"No, you can't. Just assume they've seen you and be ready. When you make landfall, you will enter a large body of water, which the Irish call the Lough Feabhail. After a day's sail the waterway narrows to a mighty river. At a bend in this river lies a rich monastery, and Murchad's stronghold is not far from it. I suggest you attack the monastery to draw Murchad out." Ivar nodded to a burly warrior seated nearby. "Kol can guide you."

Kol was square shaped, as broad as he was tall. His arms were thick as tree trunks, his fists hammerheads. He sported a head of sandy hair and a full beard to match. "My men will be glad to go along. There should be plenty of booty left in the valley since your father's raid failed."

Harald's eyes widened at the insult and he half rose. Ivar laid a hand on his shoulder and gently pressed him back onto his seat.

"I meant no insult," said Kol with a grin.

Ivar took a conciliatory tone. "Stay with us a few days while Kol readies his ship. We will treat you well."

As the evening grew late, Gudrun rose with the other women.

"Lady Ragnhild, I would be pleased to host you and your women in the bower."

"Thank you, Lady, we are most grateful." She rose with her shield-maidens and followed her hostess.

Within the turf-roofed bower, Gudrun's women made room for them on the sleeping benches while Gudrun retired to her own chamber. She did not invite Ragnhild to join her, which was just as well. Ragnhild was happy to sleep among her shield-maidens.

She woke in the night, needing to relieve herself after all the ale she had consumed. She rose quietly and let herself out.

When she had visited the latrine behind the hall, she wandered down the beach trail to check on *Raider Bride*. The night was warm, the sky was dark and studded with stars.

As Ragnhild approached the shore she was surprised to hear movement. She watched from the shadows as a dozen men slid a small karvi into the water. They splashed aboard and took up oars while others watched them depart.

"Safe travels. We will meet you on the Lough Feabhail," a voice called low from the men on the shore.

Gravel crunched as the men came back up the trail. Ragnhild shrank into the shadow of a stone marker as they passed by. She couldn't make out their faces in the dark. Who were they, and why had they sent a boat on ahead, in the dark of night?

She waited until they had been gone quite a while before she returned to the bower and fell asleep, staring into the embers of the longfire.

In the morning, she confronted her brother in private. "A ship departed for Ireland last night."

Harald looked at her impatiently. "Yes, we sent a party ahead to scout for us. We will meet them when we arrive, and they will report on conditions."

"Why did they leave in the middle of the night? And why wasn't I informed?"

Harald rolled his eyes. "They launched when the tide was favorable. It was a small boat and as you have seen the tidal currents can be strong among the skerries. It was something we discussed before you got here. There was no opportunity to tell you."

This all was plausible, but it prickled at her that Harald had not thought she needed to be consulted. It was obvious that he still considered her a child. When she proved herself in battle that would change.

True to his word, Ivar feasted them for the next two nights as they and Kol readied their ships. In Ragnhild's mind they drew the preparations out longer than was needed, but everyone seemed to be having a good time. She tried to restrain her impatience to be on her way to Ireland and battle. She could hardly wait to see the look of grudging admiration on Harald's face when she crushed the Irishmen.

CHAPTER 6

Brough of Birsay, Orkney Island

Finally Kol was ready to depart. *Raider Bride* and *Battle Swan* followed Kol's ship, *Sea Steed*, out of the island's shelter. Behrt was glad the weather was flat calm when the little fleet got underway. He'd made this trip twice, first as a lad with his brothers, the second time just the year before when he returned to the land of his birth. He knew the islands were fraught with skerries and treacherous currents.

Behrt stood at the rail while the crew plied their oars. *I'm of no more use on a ship than a hunk of rock. I should not have insisted on coming along—I should have stayed by the fire where I'm not in the way.*

"I'll be lookout," he announced, looking to Ragnhild for approval. She gave a nod, and he took up his station in the bow, glad to be taking an active part.

He scanned the waters for submerged rocks and tide rips,

using a white signal flag to point out hazards as they worked their way south through the Orkney Islands.

Though there was no wind, the hard-running tide flushed the ships between the islands, allowing the rowers to rest their oars while Ragnhild kept *Raider Bride* on course with the steering oar. Behrt struggled to guide her through the maelstrom of submerged rocks and riptides in the wake of the other two ships. The strong currents took hold of the keel and spun them one way and then the other. Behrt's admiration for Ragnhild grew as she maneuvered with the expertise of someone wise to the ways of tides. Neither over- nor under-correcting, she managed to keep *Raider Bride* on course.

After several intense hours, the current gradually slackened and Behrt's shoulders relaxed. The crew fitted their oars and rowed hard through the slack. Behrt still kept a close lookout, but it was much easier to navigate the shoals without the current threatening to dash them on the rocks.

By midafternoon, the tide strengthened against them, and Kol led the little fleet to a deserted cove where they dropped anchor to wait out the contrary current.

"It's no good trying to buck the tide in these islands," Kol said. "We save our strength now and make up the distance when the tide is with us."

They stayed on board, eating a cold meal of dried meat and flatbread washed down with a ration of ale, and took turns napping. Though he was exhausted, Behrt volunteered to stay awake, watching the current rage against the rocks. As soon as it slackened, he woke the crew, and they raised anchor and fitted their oars once more. Through the long summer evening, the ships skimmed across the calm water. Behrt stared into the darkening depths, straining to make out submerged hazards until the shadows played tricks with the rocks and Kol directed them into another cove for the night.

They slept aboard that night and spent the next working their way through the islands, then put into a protected bay that evening. They beached the ships, making camp and building a proper fire to cook a hot meal of barley porridge and salt pork. Afterward, the crews lingered around the campfire, sipping their ale in silence, too worn out from the day's work for their usual chatter.

Behrt sought his hudfat as soon as he'd finished eating. His wounds throbbed and his muscles ached, and it was a relief to stretch out wrapped in warm fleece on unmoving land. Despite the pain, he fell into sleep like a stone dropped into a well.

Ragnhild shook him awake at dawn. Behrt struggled into a sitting position, stifling a groan as his old injuries seared to life.

Ragnhild held out a bowl of steaming porridge. "You're pulling your weight. Don't worry." Behrt accepted the bowl, wondering if she really meant it or if she was just trying to make him feel better.

The porridge warmed him and strength flowed into his stiff limbs. He climbed out of his sheepskin and set to work, helping strike camp and load the ship. After a few jagged moments, the pain ebbed and the stiffness eased. By the time they shoved off the beach, he was feeling almost vigorous. He heaved himself aboard without a struggle.

It was a fine morning. Sail set, they skirted the rugged north coast of the land of Alba before heading southwest to thread through the archipelago that sheltered the southern passage. There was little wind and the crew plied their oars once more, though the currents here were less perverse than in the Orkneys. Dolphins and seabirds of all descriptions teemed the waters, reaping the rich harvest of the sea.

Late in the day they broke out of the islands into ocean swells and hoisted sail to a good northerly breeze, running across the open water. Behrt searched the coastline until he sighted a tiny island. "There is the sacred Isle of Iona," he said. "The blessed

Colm Cille sailed there from Ireland with twelve brethren in a hide boat."

"In a hide boat?" Ragnhild scoffed. "That's impossible."

"Nay, the Irish currachs are a seaworthy craft, and Colm Cille's monks were a doughty crew. And God protected them."

"He must have," said Ragnhild, shaking her head as she stared at the rugged seaway.

"When the saint and his brethren arrived, an established druid colony already existed on the island," Behrt continued. "Colm Cille converted them all to Christians and founded a great monastery."

"Which the Norsemen love to plunder," said Svein.

Behrt's elation soured as he stared at the island. "It's true. Seventeen years ago, Norse raiders attacked Iona. They burned the settlement and martyred sixty-three monks."

"What kind of plunder?" Ragnhild asked.

"Iona held many treasures, and the greatest scriptorium ever established."

"A scriptorium?"

Behrt nodded, rapt again. He imagined landing on that island, being welcomed by the brethren. "The monks create beautiful manuscripts on calfskin scraped smooth as baby skin. It is writing, like the runes, but far more glorious. The volumes are painted like the carvings on the high seat pillars, full of serpents and angels in colors made from precious pigments, lapis lazuli, silver and gold. Each page is a precious work." He cut off his words, thinking of greedy Norse hands desecrating the sacred works.

Behrt watched Iona dwindle into the distance. A longing rose in his chest, threatening to choke him. When distance smudged the sacred isle into the land, he swallowed hard and turned his face to the south.

The wind stayed steady from the north and the ships made

good time. They stopped one more night on an island before crossing the North Passage.

The breeze held favorable throughout the ocean crossing from the land of the Dal Riata, the fearsome Irish sea kings. Behrt kept his station on the bow, though he did not need to watch for hazards. He spent the long day peering into the distance, and was the first to sight the familiar cliffs of Ireland rising from the sea. A thin column of smoke rose from the top, the only sign of the hillfort high above.

They turned east to skirt the north coast of Ireland, rounded the headland, and followed Kol's and Harald's ships through the narrow gap that opened into a vast estuary surrounded by low hills. The body of water broadened to the south, stretching out of sight.

"It is the Lough Feabhail," said Behrt. "Named for an ancient hero who, legend claims, drowned here. In this place, men live by the tide."

Though the inlet was completely protected from the sea, the wind against the ebb tide raised a formidable chop. They anchored in the lee of the north shore to await the turn of the tide, resting and watching the water. Late in the afternoon the tide slackened, and the waves began to lay down. Kol signaled that they should get underway.

The flood tide in harmony with the wind carried the ships south. As they sailed beneath a rugged cliff, Behrt glimpsed a stone cross silhouetted against the sky. His heart caught and he stared after it until the shape dwindled out of sight. He was home.

Near evening, Kol turned into a wooded cove, and as the little fleet entered the bay, they saw a karvi pulled up on the shore. Kol led them to beach alongside the karvi, where they were greeted by the crew of Orcadian scouts that had been sent ahead.

"There are hostiles about," the scout warned.

They lit no fire but took their meal of hardtack and smoked

fish, sharing ale as the scouts gave their report.

"South of here is the mouth of the River Feabhail, where the monastery of Daire Calgach stands. It has stout timber walls, but looks to be undefended. We've been watching and we've only seen a few Christ-followers."

Kol smiled. "That sounds like an ideal situation. At first light we'll sail down to the river and attack the monastery. Their signal fire will draw Murchad out of his fortress. Get a good night's sleep. Tomorrow we fight."

Behrt's insides roiled, and he fought down nausea. He had not grasped the reality of this before. How could he be part of an attack on a house of God?

Without a fire to warm them, the crews rolled out their sheepskins early. Behrt approached Ragnhild, his stomach a knot of worry. "Lady, I can't take part in the attack on the monastery."

"What did you think we were going to do here, sacrifice a goat?" said Ragnhild, not hiding the exasperation in her voice. "You shouldn't have come along if you felt that way."

Bile rose in Behrt's chest, choking off his words. She was right.

Ragnhild sighed and shook her head. "When we attack, you can stay with the boats."

Behrt nodded and retired to his hudfat. But in spite of his exhaustion, he tossed and turned as if he were still at sea. At last he rose, knowing what he must do. He would make off in the dark and warn the monastery. Like the others, he'd gone to bed fully dressed. Now he pulled on his boots and strapped on his sword, hiding the weapon beneath his cloak.

"Call of nature?" asked the man on watch as he passed.

Behrt nodded and stumbled off into the bushes. It was far too dark to travel, and he wasn't sure of the way to the monastery, or even how far it was, but he needed to try. He circled through the scrub and made his way down to the beach. If he followed the shoreline, he would eventually reach the monastery. Whether he'd get there in time, he couldn't know. He had several hours' head start on the ships, though once they launched, they'd probably outpace him.

He set off along the water's edge. As he walked, his thoughts did battle. What would his shipmates do when they found him gone? Why was he going to warn the Irish, the very people who had rejected him? Was he really going to betray those who had taken him in, who had accepted him as one of their own when no one else would?

Or at least try to betray them, for though he walked for hours, when dawn took him, the monastery of Daire Calgach was nowhere in sight.

Behrt had been sure that if he followed the river south, he'd come to the monastery, though he had no idea how far it was from where they'd made camp. He'd been a fool to strike out on his own in the night—but what else could he have done? He had to try to warn the monks of the impending attack.

As the sun rose, he found himself among farmsteads in their familiar ring-shaped enclosures. Smoke rose from the thatched roofs of the round wattle houses. Inside, he knew, the women would be preparing barley porridge over the fire. Behrt's stomach growled at the thought. In his fraught state of mind, he hadn't considered bringing food or even water. He carried his weapons and not much more.

A boy herding sheep halted to stare at him.

"A fine morning to you, lad," Behrt said. The boy's eyes grew round. Dressed as a heathen warrior, a sword hanging from his belt, Behrt realized he must present a fearful sight. He softened his look with a smile. "I mean no harm to you and yours. I wonder only if you could tell me how far the monastery of Daire Calgach might be?"

The lad continued to stare, speechless, then bolted toward the farmstead, his charges forgotten.

Behrt waited. The lad would fetch his father. He could ask the man how far the monastery was, and perhaps even get some breakfast.

Soon the boy appeared over the rise. Behind him came a man Behrt assumed was his father. The man brandished his hoe like a weapon, and no wonder. He was meeting an armed Norseman.

But over the rise came more men. A crowd of them, all wielding farm implements.

Behrt considered running, but where could he go? His injuries made him slow, and this open country held no cover. He held his arms up, showing that his sword was still sheathed, and waited for them.

They came at him on a run.

"I mean no harm," Behrt shouted.

When they didn't slow down, Behrt drew his sword. The first man reached him and swung his hoe. Behrt dodged and took the blow on his shoulder and slashed his sword low, catching his attacker in the legs, bringing him down. But before Behrt could recover, the others were on him. He hacked into them and managed to land a few more blows, but there were too many of them. He heard screams, but he realized they were his own as he was pummeled with hard wood and iron. He collapsed under the blows that kept coming until he could feel no more.

RAGNHILD JOLTED awake at first light. She stared across the broad gray expanse of water and smudge of hills in the distance, blurred by haze. Waterfowl rose squawking from the shallows.

Today she would prove herself in battle against the man who dared to buy her. She would enhance her reputation, claim her inheritance, and gain her freedom once and for all.

There was movement on the beach. Harald's men and the Orcadians were already striking camp. She scrambled out of her hudfat and hurried to rouse her crew.

"There's no time for porridge," she said, trying to keep the excitement from her voice.

Behrt's sheepskin was empty. She wasn't surprised that the Christian was up already. The poor man had probably not slept much, with such a dilemma roiling in his mind.

The crew munched on flatbread while they rolled up their hudfat. They scurried to the shore in time to launch *Raider Bride* alongside the other ships.

"Where's the Christian?" asked Einar.

Ragnhild realized Behrt had not returned.

"He's betrayed us," said Svein. "He's gone to warn the monastery."

Ragnhild's heart lurched. She should have realized he was on the verge of such an action. Another failure of leadership on her part.

"Don't worry," said Einar. "His warning will only help us. Our purpose is to bring Murchad out of his fortress, to do battle."

In spite of Einar's reassurance, Ragnhild still seethed at her poor judgment and inability to control her crew.

"You didn't want to bring him," said Einar. "Åsa overruled you. Your instincts were sound. And no harm done."

What Einar said was true. Ragnhild allowed herself to feel a little better. She mounted *Raider Bride's* prow beast, a wild horse's head, with pride while the crew ran out their oars. She made her way back to the stern, took the helm, and looked over at her brother.

Harald showed his teeth and the race began. The rowers put their backs into every stroke as the ships bit into the opposing current. *Raider Bride's* crew was determined to keep pace with the two longer ships and they succeeded, while the scouts' karvi trailed a bit behind.

They traversed the western shore of the lough in a fine mist, sighting fisherman's shacks and small farmsteads clustered along the shore, with occasional ring-shaped fortresses set on commanding bluffs.

Ragnhild eyed the settlements. Each steading was encircled by woven withy fences, some mounted on earthworks. Within the enclosures rose curious round structures crowned by dome-shaped thatched roofs. Outside the fences, cattle and sheep grazed in gently rolling pastures. It looked like fine raiding country.

The estuary narrowed, intensifying the current. They struggled against it for an hour, until the waterway broadened into a fast-flowing, serpentine river.

Raider Bride's prow beast was even with the bigger ships when they rounded a bend and a more significant fortification appeared. A sturdy wooden palisade rose from an earthen embankment, punctuated by a stout oak gate that faced the river.

"This is Daire Calgach, the monastery," shouted Kol.

The monastery stood on a hill that at first appeared to be an island. On the crown of the hill beside the fortification rose an impressive grove of ancient oaks. As they drew near, Ragnhild could see that the back side of the hill was surrounded by nearly impenetrable marshland.

Kol turned his bow toward shore, Harald following in his wake.

"Heave!" Ragnhild shouted, determined to be the first to land. Her crew dug their oar-blades deep into the water as they rowed crosscurrent. They managed to edge ahead of the other ships, reaching the shore first.

Heart beating hard, Ragnhild drew her sword and leaped over the side. Kol and Harald landed just after her, and they raced up the beach toward the walls, leaving their crews to drag the longships up the beach. The two men's legs were longer than Ragnhild's, and they tore up the hill. She managed to keep up by sheer will, but she was growing winded.

Harald and Kol stopped at the gate, gasping for breath. Ragnhild came to a halt gratefully while they waited for the crews to catch up.

Kol pounded on the gate, shouting something in a foreign tongue. Ragnhild was surprised that he would even bother. It seemed unlikely that defenseless holy men would open to marauders. The gates didn't look that sturdy. She scanned the hillside for a suitable log that might serve as a battering ram.

To her amazement, the gates creaked open. Steel flashed and her stomach dropped. Instead of cowering monks, an army crowded the entrance, bristling with spear tips.

Ragnhild tamped down panic and turned to Kol. "What is our plan?"

Kol did not reply. He looked to Harald, who avoided her eyes.

Her heart went into freefall as the horde of Irish marched out and encircled the three of them, cutting them off from their boat crews. Ragnhild turned to the boats, mind racing as she calculated the odds of a fight. Her crew was already striding up the beach, shields up and spears leveled, but Kol's and Harald's men stood by the boats.

She looked to her brother, but Harald was staring at the enemy.

The throng of Irish parted to let a tall, broad-shouldered warrior stride through. He was the only one clad in a mail shirt over a yellow linen tunic, and his knee-length, multi-colored mantle was finely woven, fastened with a massive silver brooch. His hair hung to his shoulders, straight and black as a crow's wing, and he wore a golden torc about his neck. His chin was clean-shaven, but his black moustache was long and full. A stout man came behind him, lugging an oaken chest.

They halted before Harald. Ragnhild watched in shock as her brother came forward and took the chest.

Harald inclined his head to the black-haired warrior. At last her brother met her eyes with the flicker of a smile. "Sister, here is your husband."

CHAPTER 7

Daire Calgach Monastery

The fullness of her brother's plan fell on her like a hammer. All this time, since sending Orlyg to Tromøy, withholding her inheritance, the trip to Ireland… He had never intended to avenge their father. Instead, he'd lured her into a trap she thought she'd escaped long ago.

"You planned this!"

Harald gave her a sickly smile. "I knew you would take the bait. All I had to do was forbid you to come along."

"You treacherous bastard," Ragnhild hissed. She peered through the thicket of Irish spears. Her eyes met Einar's as the full extent of the betrayal dawned.

"Flee!" she shouted.

Einar only hesitated for an instant. Then he pivoted, driving the crew down the beach toward *Raider Bride.* Svein had already drawn his sword.

Harald turned to bark an order. Ragnhild's knife was flying

through the air before anyone could react. This time Harald dodged. The blade struck the oak treasure chest, quivering with a solid thunk.

It delayed him long enough for her crew to reach *Raider Bride*. Moving as one, they hauled the ship into the waves.

"Stop them!" Harald shouted. But *Raider Bride* was already in midstream, oars run out, riding the river's swift northerly current.

Ragnhild watched them gain a healthy lead before she turned to face the Irish leader.

He was well-muscled and moved with energy, but the lines on his face marked his age as perhaps thirty.

Ragnhild pulled off her helmet and glared in challenge. His gaze raked her from head to foot, lingering on her tattooed throat. He shook his long hair back as a delighted smile spread across his face.

He bowed. "Lady, I am Murchad mac Maele Duin, king of Aileach and lord of the Cenel nEoghan," he said in perfect Norse.

She drew herself up tall. "I am Ragnhild, daughter of King Solvi of Rogaland."

Murchad's smile widened. "My promised bride, come at last."

Ragnhild swallowed her fury and said nothing, struggling to keep her face composed. She had fought a war to avoid this marriage her father had arranged, only to be betrayed by her brother. There was no doubt Murchad had expected her. The Orcadian scouts had ensured that, while Ivar delayed them on Orkney. What a fool she was.

If Murchad thinks he's getting a wife, then he's the fool.

Yet she realized that her life and the lives of her crew depended on her cooperation with this Irishman. This was his country, and he could hunt them down if he wished.

She met his eyes. "Leave my crew in peace and I will come willingly."

"You'll come one way or another no matter what I do."

Murchad's eyes sparkled dangerously. He nodded at two men, who came forward and tried to take her sword. She tightened her grip on the pommel and glowered at the men, who hesitated, looking to their king uncertainly.

Murchad's grin widened. "You need not fear, my lady. Your crew is too small a force to trouble us. I will not pursue them. But I cannot speak for your brother." He jutted his chin toward the beach.

Ragnhild followed his gaze. Harald and Kol had reached their boats. They shoved off and rowed after *Raider Bride*, which was already vanishing around a bend in the river. Ragnhild hoped they had gained enough distance to elude her brother. But where would they hide? They were strangers here, unable to speak the language, marked as raiders hated and feared by the local people. They could expect no help.

There was nothing she could do for them right now. She turned back to Murchad.

"Your sword, lady."

Ragnhild hesitated, but it was clear he'd take it from her by force, if necessary. She reluctantly offered him the hilt.

He took hold of the weapon. As Ragnhild let go of Lady's Servant, a chill of despair bled through her. She quickly brought her hand to her side so her enemies would not see it tremble.

"Come." Murchad took her arm and gently led her through the gates into a yard littered with a scattering of the small, round huts crowned with conical thatched roofs. Squawking chickens milled about the yard, pecking for seed. In one corner stood a lone rectangular structure built of stone, though its roof was thatched like the others. The ornate stone cross in the foreyard marked it as a Christ temple. Inside, no doubt, lay golden treasures, there for the taking. Ragnhild noted that the door stood open and unguarded.

Within a fence of woven twigs, three men dressed in coarse-spun robes tended an herb garden. As they bent to their task, sunlight glinted on the tops of their heads, which had been shaved in front from ear to ear.

Ragnhild eyed the wooden palisade that rose far above her head. Could she scale it? The timbers looked rough, promising good purchase—and slivers.

Murchad smiled at her and said, "I wish we could linger here, but we must depart immediately. Our wedding feast awaits at my fortress, Aileach."

Hope sparked in Ragnhild. With luck, Einar had gotten *Raider Bride* away from Harald and would find a place to hide and wait for her downriver. She needed to escape and join them, then rain Hel's fire on her brother. If Murchad was taking her out of here, she might have a chance. Perhaps she would find an opportunity to loot this temple first.

Murchad took hold of her elbow and guided her across the yard. The iron beneath his gentle grip took her by surprise, and she found herself going along like a well-trained horse.

The Irish horde had gathered beside a herd of shaggy ponies. Murchad led her to a small brown one, held by a skinny boy who stared at her, round-eyed.

"Lady, please accept Brunaidh as a wedding gift," said Murchad. "You will find her a biddable mount."

Ragnhild brightened. On horseback, she'd have a better chance of escape. As she approached, the pony turned its head to regard her with soft brown eyes. Ragnhild clucked her tongue and murmured softly. Brunaidh's ears twitched with interest. She stroked the pony's neck, then stopped short.

The horse wore no saddle. There was only a thick blanket across her back.

Ragnhild was a good rider, but she was accustomed to saddles with stirrups. How did the Irish mount their horses? Covertly, she watched Murchad with his own horse, a dapple gray. From a dead standstill, the Irish king sprang into the air, legs scissoring, to land lightly on his horse's back, squarely on the blanket. His warriors followed suit, seeming to fly onto their mounts.

Ragnhild quailed. She was going to make a fool of herself in front of these Irish. If it increased her chance of escape, so be it. Taking a deep breath, she sized up the situation. Brunaidh's back was low and broad. She ought to be able to at least get up there, if not gracefully. Feigning confidence, she took the reins from the boy and choked. It was a single rein, attached to the top of the bridle's nose band. Sneaking a glance at the other riders, she saw that they led their rein straight back over the horse's forehead.

Gripping the rein in her left hand, she drew in a deep breath and laid her right on Brunaidh's withers. The small horse stood complacently. Ragnhild hooked her arm around the pony's neck, gave a hop and swung her right leg up, managing to heave herself onto Brunaidh's back. In the process, the blanket went askew, and she had an awkward moment rearranging it between her legs. The result was not graceful, but at least she was mounted.

Murchad smiled. "I will teach you how to ride, *a mhuirin*." Ragnhild felt her color rise, completing her humiliation.

The boy handed her a long stick. She took it and surreptitiously watched Murchad cluck and tap his pony lightly on the flank with his own stick. His gray moved forward obediently. Ragnhild copied his movement, and Brunaidh stepped out with the other horses. Ragnhild felt almost giddy with success.

Murchad led them out through the gates, his warriors crowding close around her. They skirted the wall to the north, and as they came to the western side, Ragnhild's hopes sank. The monastery and its oak grove stood on a hill that was little more than an island, fronted by the river and backed by a marsh.

The warriors hustled her onto a narrow wood-planked causeway that crossed the bog to higher ground to the northwest. Ragnhild surveyed the landscape. The marshland stretched for miles in all directions, providing no cover. Even if she could break away, with her inexperience in Irish horsemanship, her captors would ride her down in no time—if she didn't sink into the bog. She could only go along helplessly, watching for an opportunity.

They had ridden a little more than an hour when the causeway gave onto higher, firmer ground. A road led through a landscape patterned with fields and ring-shaped enclosures, some corralling cattle or sheep.

They mounted another knoll crowned by a massive earthen rampart. As they drew nearer, Ragnhild saw that the stone-faced bank rose twice the height of a man and was surrounded by a deep ditch. These fortifications were far more substantial than those of the monastery. Once inside, she'd never escape.

The gate swung open, and before them stood another embankment with an oak gate manned by two warriors. The warriors opened the gate, bowing to Murchad as he passed. Inside the road narrowed, constricted by a waist-high rock fence that terminated at a narrow doorway set in a stone rampart. This wall was twice as high as the other two. Armed men watched them from the top.

As they approached, the door creaked open to darkness. Ragnhild shivered as Murchad took hold of Brunaidh's bridle and guided them inside.

They entered a narrow, stone-lined passage that left barely enough room for the two of them to ride side by side. The dank walls smelled of must. Warriors crowded in behind, barring any escape.

Ragnhild's heart beat wildly as Murchad propelled her along. She gripped Brunaidh's mane and fixed her gaze on the rectangle of light that shone ahead, watching it grow larger until at last they burst into daylight.

Her hands shook with relief to be out of the tunnel. Before them lay a broad courtyard teeming with people and livestock. Shrieks and squawks accompanied children and fowl as they scurried about the gravel-paved yard. An immense structure dominated the enclosure. It was nearly as big as a Norse chieftain's hall, but perfectly circular in shape rather than oblong, and crowned by a conical, thatched roof shaped like a pointed hat. It made the building look like some sort of magical creature that might rise up and walk off at any moment.

A dozen or so smaller buildings crouched in the shelter of the roundhouse like the chicks of an enormous hen. A manure pile ripened in the corner of the yard, transmitting a rich, earthy stink. In the eastern corner stood the rectangular shape of a Christ temple, fronted by an ornately carved stone cross like the one at the monastery.

The Irish dismounted. Ragnhild stayed on Brunaidh's back, clutching the rein, until Murchad took hold of the pony's bridle. He reached up, encircling Ragnhild's waist with one arm, and gently drew her off the pony's back. Ragnhild tensed against his grip and found he was like a firmly-rooted tree.

The same boy who had brought Brunaidh to her this morning came forward. He peeled the rein from her sweating hand and led the pony off with the others. Keeping a firm grip on Ragnhild, Murchad ushered her along a stone-lined path toward the gaping door of the great hall. The exterior walls glowed with whitewashed wattle, and the stout wooden doorframe was carved with strange runes.

A man-at-arms stood aside and they crossed the kerbstone. Inside, the walls were whitewashed as well, lending the dim room a welcome brightness. The roof peak vanished into darkness, supported by massive poles carved with more runes and inlaid with bronze. Fine tapestries hung from the beams, studded with gleaming silver and gold brooches set with precious stones. The room was filled with wealth, there for the taking.

The flagstone floor was strewn with fragrant rushes. A fire sulked in a stone hearth at the center of the room, but the smoke rose into the ceiling's high peak and found its way out through the thatch.

Ragnhild identified the high seat on a platform beyond the hearth. Deep benches lined the walls, separated by woven partitions to form compartments for those who slept in the hall. Another row of benches circled the hearth. The vast room could accommodate a sizeable hird, as many as any Norse chieftain's hall.

Murchad led Ragnhild past the hearth to a low doorway on the far end of the room. They ducked through into another, smaller building, round and thatched like the first. In the center of the room, an iron cauldron simmered on a tripod over the stone hearth. Bed alcoves, again separated by wattle panels, were tucked against the walls.

A short, middle-aged woman stood beside the hearth. She wore a green linen gown belted at the waist and clutched her saffron woolen shawl close to her throat, staring at Ragnhild as she might a wild beast.

"This is Fiona," said Murchad with a smile, ignoring the woman's obvious distress. "She will serve you. She does not speak Norse, but I am sure the two of you will make yourselves understood. I have ordered her to teach you to speak our language." He beamed at the Irishwoman, who managed to scowl while inclining her head respectfully. Her apparent displeasure seemed not to trouble Murchad in the least.

Murchad peered around the room. "There are more women to attend you. I am surprised they are not here to greet you." He spoke sharply to Fiona, who replied in fraught tones. Murchad's brows drew together and his voice sharpened, sending Fiona scurrying out the back door.

"She's gone to get the other women. As I said, there will be no trouble making your needs clear to them." Murchad's tone was ominous, and Ragnhild felt a twinge of sympathy for the women, mingled with a dread of being left with them.

"I will leave you to rest and refresh yourself." Murchad departed. Relief swept over her. It was the first time she'd been alone since her capture. The respite was short-lived, for Fiona crept in, dragging three young women with her. They looked to be close to Ragnhild's age, while Fiona was several years older. They huddled together, staring at her.

Ragnhild longed to send them away. Fear and exhaustion battled thirst and hunger within her. Fiona approached her and reached out to tug on her clothes, saying something in Irish. Ragnhild realized that her salt-encrusted battle jacket chafed unbearably. She unbuckled the leather strap and shucked off the stiff quilted garment, allowing her chest to expand with a deep breath for the first time that day. The wool coverlet on the bed looked soft and warm. She sat, sinking into the feather mattress, and pulled off her ankle boots with a sigh.

Fiona approached with a bowl of wash water and set it on the small table beside the bed, then backed away. Ragnhild plunged her hands into the warm water, bathing her face and neck, dissolving the sweat and grime. She undid her salt-stiff braids and brought out the antler comb that hung from her belt. As she smoothed the snarls from her hair, the dull ache in her head gradually eased.

Another young woman entered through the back door, bearing a jug of ale and a wooden plate piled with oat cakes. Ragnhild's mouth was parched and her stomach tight with hunger. She seized the food and fell on it like a wolf. It occurred to her that her behavior would do nothing to improve the Irish-women's opinion of her. Perhaps that was for the best, she thought with a grin.

After Ragnhild had demolished the cakes and ale, Fiona emerged from her alcove, a linen gown in her arms.

"I'll not wear that rag," Ragnhild said in Norse, with an emphatic shake of her head.

Fiona replied sharply and held the gown up as if to bring it over Ragnhild's head.

"I said no!" Ragnhild seized the garment and threw it at the Irishwoman's feet.

"*Finn gaill!*" Fiona's tone conveyed outrage. She picked up the gown and stormed out, slamming the oaken door behind her.

Ragnhild sat on her bed, staring at the whitewashed walls, ignoring the silent women.

A little while later, the door opened and Fiona walked in, carrying a clean linen tunic and woolen breeks.

A peace offering.

Ragnhild had won this battle, small as it was. She rose from the bed and inclined her head in what she hoped Fiona would see as a gracious gesture.

"Thank you." Ragnhild took the clothes and dressed, wondering what boy might be going naked.

Now that she was fed and clothed, the warmth of the room stifled her. She had to get out. She strode resolutely to the back door, Fiona and the others trailing behind. Ragnhild gave the door a yank. It flew open, flooding the room with the golden light of late afternoon.

The women followed her out into the yard, pointing at things and gabbling in their language. Ragnhild ignored them. She surveyed the yard, bounded by the stone rampart. A wooden platform ran the circumference of the wall, and it could be reached by a flight of stairs. Ragnhild hurried to the steps and climbed up, while the women clustered below, watching and chattering in their language.

As she stepped out onto the platform, a sentry confronted her. She gave the man her fiercest scowl. He drew back, confusion on his features. She could see him weigh her intrusion against her status as Murchad's future queen. Apparently her rank won out, for he smiled uncertainly and moved aside.

She stared out over the countryside. The fortress surrounded by bog. To the south, the land sloped gently toward the river, and she could make out the monastery in the distance.

Far to the east rose a distant mountain range, and the north was checkered with variegated green fields and circular enclosures.

"It's beautiful country."

Murchad stood beside her, gazing raptly across the fields, passion for his land inscribed on his face.

"My father won this country from the Conaills through many bloody battles," he said. "In the end it cost him his life, and the lives of many brave men. My father burned the monastery of Daire Calgach to the ground the year before I was born. What you saw today has been rebuilt by my clan. This fortress was Cenel Conaill's as well, but they did not fortify it well enough to withstand my father. They never stop trying to take it back, though. Two years ago they nearly succeeded when they killed our king, my foster father. But I overcame them and avenged his death."

"Then you understand that I must avenge my father's death," said Ragnhild.

Murchad bared his teeth at her. "I paid your father's weregild to your brother along with your bride price."

Ragnhild's heart slammed against her chest, hard and painful. She reeled away from him, keeping her face down to hide the furious tears that blurred her vision. All she'd done to avoid this fate was in vain. She had run away, crossed the mountains alone on skis. She'd fought a war against her father, raided his treasure. All to be duped like a common fool and sold as a peace-cow by her own brother. And now to learn that Harald had taken compensation for her father as well, cutting her out of her portion yet again.

"Wait," Murchad called after her, but she rushed down the steps and stormed blindly across the yard.

Those Hel-cursed Irishwomen were waiting. They followed her, faces puckered with concern. She glowered at them and they backed away, but when she moved on they trailed her in a timid little cluster.

She halted and turned on them. "Can't you leave me alone?" she shouted. They drew back for an instant, but then Fiona came forward and took her elbow. The Irishwoman pulled gently, speaking in cajoling tones, and Ragnhild found herself being towed along toward the women's quarters.

Fiona led her inside, guided her to her bed, and gently coaxed her onto the down mattress. The sweet aroma of dried herbs rose as Ragnhild settled into the soft depths. She shivered and Fiona pulled the wool blanket up, tucking it under her chin.

The Irishwoman crossed to the cauldron and drew a cup of something steaming and fragrant. She brought it to Ragnhild, murmuring in soothing tones.

Ragnhild was about to hurl the wooden cup in the Irishwoman's face, but something in Fiona's voice stopped her. Instead, she accepted the cup. She inhaled the herbal scent and sipped the hot liquid cautiously. The brew warmed her stomach, a warmth that spread up into her chest. Her heart gradually slowed its gallop, and her breath calmed.

Fiona backed away. The shadows rustled as the Irishwomen settled into their alcoves, calling softly to each other in their lilting tongue. The empty cup fell from Ragnhild's fingers, but her arms were too heavy to pick it up.

Her eyes drifted closed.

CHAPTER 8

River Feabhail

R*aider Bride* rode the river current north. As soon as the ship spilled into the Lough Feabhail, her crew wasted no time in raising sail. Einar peered anxiously at their wake. Harald and Kol were out of sight but couldn't be far behind.

All through the night they sailed up the middle of the lough, and when dawn came Einar could make out three sails in the distance.

"Not far enough," said Thorgeir. Einar nodded grimly. He was still trying to process what had taken place. Harald had given Ragnhild to the Irishman in exchange for a chest of silver, keeping their father's bargain with the Irish king. That much was clear. That it was pre-arranged was certain, pointing to Kol's scout. Einar shook his head. Time to think on this when they were in a safe place.

It took most of the day to traverse the lough, and *Raider Bride's* crew was exhausted by the time they sighted the entrance. Einar knew they must rest before setting out into the open sea. He directed the rowers to skirt the coast where the shoreline was indented with wooded coves, hoping to hide in the trees. He passed by the first estuaries, winding around bends to put some cover between them and their pursuers.

It was near dark when they dropped sail and rowed into a promising bay, fed by a creek that was sheltered by overhanging branches. The creek was just deep enough to pull the longship in beneath the foliage. The crew made fast to the trunks and crawled into their hudfat, asleep within minutes.

Einar hoped their mast didn't stick up too noticeably above the scrubby trees. He took the first watch, propping himself against the hull, blinking furiously to keep his eyes open.

He was grateful when Svein relieved him after a short time.

"Couldn't sleep." Einar knew Svein was lying, but he lay down thankfully, knowing he'd be more useful after a little rest.

It seemed like he'd barely gotten his eyes closed when Svein hissed. Einar bolted upright. He peered through the branches at the moonlit water as *Battle Swan* scudded into the bay, followed by Kol's ship and the scout's karvi. Clutching their weapons, Einar and Svein watched in tense silence as the three ships made a turn around the bay, praying that *Raider Bride* was well enough hidden by the foliage and darkness.

Einar hoped it wouldn't come to a fight, but if it did, *Raider Bride's* crew had the advantage of a little rest. Their pursuers had to be as tired as they were. But Harald and Kol had a lot more men.

The ships completed their reconnaissance and to Einar's horror dropped their anchors at the entrance to the bay. They were positioned so that they effectively blocked the only escape route.

Einar held a whispered council with Thorgeir and Svein. They agreed all they could do was wait until moonset and make a run for it. Time crept by as Einar and Svein kept watch while

Thorgeir rested. Even though the pursuing ships had raised their awnings and their crews must be sleeping as soundly as his own people, Einar knew he would be taking a huge risk trying to sneak past them. The enemy ships would certainly have lookouts. With their superior numbers, if they caught *Raider Bride*, it would be all over. But if he waited for daylight, they would be seen for sure.

Like a mouse in a hole, they watched the ships.

When the moon had set, Einar and Svein wakened the crew, hushing them into silence and pointing out the three ships anchored across the entrance. Einar was betting that if Kol and Harald had set a lookout, those men would have succumbed to sleep by now. After all, they thought they were alone in the bay, and they had no reason to be afraid of attack in this isolated place.

The crew slipped the mooring lines and eased out of the creek, trying not to rustle the branches as they pulled the ship along. When they broke out into the bay, they cautiously fitted their oars and dipped the blades in the water, barely disturbing the surface.

Raider Bride ghosted across the bay. As they neared the entrance, they had to pass close to the other ships.

Einar watched the anchored vessels carefully. No one stirred.

They had just passed Harald's ship and were nearly at the bay's entrance when someone's oar squeaked. The sound blared, unnaturally loud in the silent night.

The rowers froze, holding their oars and their breaths, praying the enemy had not heard.

A groggy shout sank that hope.

"Row!" Einar rasped.

Now all they could do was drive the ship as fast as they could along the shore, putting sea miles between themselves and their pursuers while the enemy fumbled awake and got underway. Einar whispered thanks to the sea goddess Ran that Harald and

Kol had set their awnings, for it would take them precious time to stow the bulky piece of heavy wool.

Outside the bay, the sea lay dark and flat as obsidian. Their oars stirred up a ghostly luminescence that seemed to reflect the stars. Einar posted a lookout on the bow, searching the darkness for rocks. In truth they were rowing blind.

He looked back. By starlight he caught the movement as one slim hull glided out of the harbor, the second close behind. He prayed to Ran that his enemies would find the submerged rocks, not he.

Raider Bride's crew had the benefit of more rest, but that was their only advantage. The enemy ships' longer waterlines and bigger crews made them inherently faster. Einar wished Ragnhild were here. Her will to win inspired her crew as he never could. For all his skill, Einar knew he was not a leader, nor did he aspire to be. He was very good at second in command.

But tonight, he must lead. He tried to imagine what Ragnhild would do, or Åsa.

The two bigger ships were gaining, the scout's karvi bringing up the rear. *Raider Bride* had made a good run of it, but it was coming on time to stand and fight, Thor help them. His shoulders slumped as he watched the crew, rowing like champions. What a shame to waste them so young.

"We can do it." He looked down to see Unn, grinning up at him as she hauled on her oar. "We can take them."

"Yes, we can," he said with conviction, though he couldn't see how.

CHAPTER 9

Aileach Cashel

"You must become Christian," said the priest in heavily accented Norse.

"Never!" Arms akimbo, Ragnhild straddled the puddle of blue silk on the floor where she had hurled it. Fiona stood in the corner of the room, white-lipped and red-faced.

"Then no marriage can take place."

"Fine!" Ragnhild eyed the priest malevolently.

"We will wed today, even if it's not blessed by the church." Murchad's voice was gentle, cajoling, as if he were trying to persuade a skittish horse to take the bit.

"Not if the bridegroom is a corpse," said Ragnhild.

Murchad's eyes widened. "*A chroi*, you must wear the silk dress and take part in the ceremony. It is our bargain."

"I told you I won't become Christian." Ragnhild glared at him.

"Nobody said anything about that. I can't imagine Father

Ferdia summoning the courage to dunk you in the river. But you must be present at the wedding ceremony. This was the agreement I had with your father, and now your brother has sworn to fulfill it. I paid your brother the honor price."

"You paid my brother! I did not agree to any of this." Ragnhild's face was hot, and she knew it was red. She clenched her fists to keep them from trembling. A fury was on her like the battle-rage. She needed to sink her knife into living flesh. Blood must flow.

"If you don't agree to this marriage, then it will not be a marriage of equals under our laws. You will forfeit your rights and power," said Murchad. When she did not reply, he continued. "A chroi, I made this alliance to protect my people."

Ragnhild struggled to bring herself to heel. The most important thing was to impose her will, to show him she was no captive slave. Her crew was out there somewhere, vulnerable. With Murchad's help, she might be able to save them.

"I will go through with the wedding, but not in the church," she said, "if you agree to let my crew go free."

"So it shall be."

"And it will be a marriage in name only."

"Understood," said Murchad. "We will be married according to the ancient laws of Ireland. I shall not require you to submit to the church's laws." He fixed her with a meaningful stare. "Nor to anything else you do not wish."

The priest must have understood at least some of what Murchad said, for he cleared his throat and began to protest.

Murchad turned to him and barked an order. The priest snapped his mouth shut. "Father Ferdia needs this alliance as much as I do. The monasteries and churches are the primary target of Norse attacks."

The old priest glowered at her and grumbled.

Murchad regarded Ragnhild, whose entire body vibrated with

rage. "I am certain that she is a virgin," he said in Norse, causing Ragnhild to bristle even more. "Come, Father, it's time to let the women do their work." He took Father Ferdia by the arm and led him to the door and all but pushed the priest outside.

Murchad turned to Ragnhild. He took her hand in a grip that was cool and light, and strangely soothing. She scowled to hide her confusion.

He rubbed the back of his neck, a slight flush on his cheeks. "There is something else I require of you."

She looked at him cautiously.

"You must spend the night in my chamber."

Her mouth dropped open.

"It's necessary." His words came in a rush. "We must appear to be husband and wife in every way. There can be no question that our marriage has been consummated." He wiped his palms on his tunic. "It will be as we agreed. I won't touch you. But we must give the appearance for the marriage to be legitimate."

Ragnhild tamped down her rage. Only patience would buy her the chance to escape and take vengeance on her brother. She closed her eyes and gave a quick nod. "I'll do it."

"Thank you, *a ghra*!" Murchad threw his arms around her and kissed her cheek. She stiffened, and he let her go. "I will see you at the ceremony." He turned and went out the door.

Fiona stepped forward and swept the silk dress off the floor. She approached Ragnhild as if she were a skittish horse, and a dangerous one at that. Ragnhild quickly shed her tunic and breeks.

When Fiona raised the dress over her head, Ragnhild fought down the desire to rip the gown from the Irishwoman's hands and fling it to the floor again. Instead she stood rigidly still. The silk cascaded over her shoulders, sending a quiver down her spine. She had not worn such a thing since before her mother died, and even then she had been forced into it.

The other women had crowded in behind Fiona, and now they descended on Ragnhild like wolves bringing down prey. They grappled with her hair, combing it out smoother than it had been in years, then started pinning and tucking, chattering as they worked. At last they stepped back to view their creation, nodding among themselves.

"What are you doing?" Ragnhild jerked her head away as Fiona tried to settle a wreath of flowers on her hair. "I feel foolish enough without bees buzzing around my head!"

Fiona shrank back with a hurt look, clutching the garland to her chest. Ragnhild felt a prick of shame for speaking so sharply. To cover it, she pivoted and marched to the door.

In the yard, the entire settlement was in the throes of preparation for the marriage celebration. Men had erected a canopy of woven branches festooned with flowers and set tables and benches around. Cauldrons simmered over outdoor fires, while hive-shaped stone ovens radiated heat and the scent of baking bread.

Ragnhild made her way across the yard, the Irishwomen scurrying in her wake. Everyone stopped what they were doing and stared as Ragnhild's attendants ushered her toward the main hall.

The door stood open to the sunlight. Through it she could see Murchad waiting, resplendent in a purple silk robe embroidered with silver thread. Around his neck gleamed the heavy gold torc. Ragnhild's hands itched to take it.

His eyes widened as he looked at her, and he smiled, sending an unwelcome warmth into her belly.

She scowled. *He is my jailer.* She strode across the stone floor and assumed her place beside him. Fiona and her women lined up next to Ragnhild, while the folk crowded in at the door.

Beside Murchad stood another man, tall and dark, dressed nearly as regally as the groom. He did not look happy, and he muttered angrily to Murchad, who cut him off with a sharp gesture and turned to Ragnhild, his expression swiftly changing to a smile.

"Lady Ragnhild, may I present my cousin, Niall mac Aeda. His father raised us both, and we are as close as brothers."

Niall frowned and bowed stiffly, to which Ragnhild gave a curt nod. They turned to face the raised table before them. Behind it stood a woman of late middle years, gray threading her russet locks. She wore a red silken gown and a multi-colored wool mantle.

Murchad bowed to the woman and took Ragnhild's hand. "Lady Ragnhild, this is the brehon Aife. She will advise us of the law and write our marriage contract."

Aife inclined her head graciously.

"She is a lawspeaker?" Ragnhild was surprised to see a woman in that role.

"Yes, that is correct," Aife answered. Ragnhild was even more amazed to hear the woman speak passable Norse.

Aife brought out a goose quill, a small pot of dark liquid, and a piece of calfskin that had been scraped smooth as a baby's behind. The brehon sharpened her quill with a tiny knife, the kind used to carve runes. But instead of carving the skin with the knife, she dipped the quill into the pot and held it poised above the calfskin.

"I understand that the bride does not understand our language," she said in Norse. "I will speak in both the bride's language and our own." She turned to Murchad. "King Murchad, son of King Maele Duin, please state the terms of marriage."

"It will be a marriage in the first degree," said Murchad. "The Lady Ragnhild is daughter of King Solvi of Lochlainn."

Aife raised her eyebrows. "You are of equal rank." She turned her gaze on Ragnhild. "Are you willing to marry this man?"

"I am." Ragnhild choked out the words, reminding herself what they would buy her.

The brehon nodded. With the sharp point of the quill, she

scratched strange-looking curved runes on the skin. The liquid in the tiny pot was nearly black in color, not red as the runes were traditionally colored. "Will this be a marriage of the man contribution, the woman contribution, or of equal contribution?"

Murchad spoke up. "It will be of the man contribution. I have paid a bride price in silver to her brother. To this marriage I bring my crannog fortress and the lands surrounding it. I bring forty sworn men, fifty head of cattle, thirty horses, fifty sheep, and a flock of geese. My wife has nothing to contribute to our marriage."

Ragnhild bristled. "I own the pony Brunaidh, a good sword, helmet, and a chain-mail shirt. Further, I own a longship with thirty-five crewmembers sworn to me, and the hall and lands of Gausel in Lochlainn." She glared at Murchad and dared him to say she did not actually have possession of these things at the moment.

Aife looked from one to the other. "It will be a marriage of equal contribution, then?" Murchad nodded. The brehon fixed Ragnhild with a solemn gaze. "Your rights under this contract are as follows: You may dismiss this man as husband, should he fail to provide for you, fail to give you children, should he take a second wife, or should he beat you and leave a mark. Your husband may divorce you for flagrant infidelity, failure to produce a child, or bad management of the home. To dissolve the marriage you must declare your intentions before witnesses. In such case, you are entitled to take with you all the property you brought with you, any gifts your husband has provided you with, and a share of the wealth of the marriage that your efforts entitle you to. Do you understand these terms, and do you agree to them?"

Ragnhild nodded. "The law is much the same in my land. I understand that I can rid myself of this man should he prove useless or annoying, and I can keep my lands and property, as well as a share of the booty we take in battle and raiding. To these conditions, I agree."

The brehon blanched, but nodded. "Close enough. I sign this as witness to your marriage contract according to the laws of Ireland." Aife scratched with a flourish, set the skin to dry. Then she began to speak to the gathering in Irish. Ragnhild caught her name, and Murchad's.

"She's reciting the terms of our marriage to the assembly," Murchad whispered.

When the brehon had finished her speech, Fiona approached, bearing a plate of oatmeal and salt, which she presented to Murchad. He dipped his hand in each and tasted them, then offered the plate to Ragnhild. She brought the oats and salt to her lips.

The brehon picked up a chalice and offered it to Murchad. He drank, then handed it to Ragnhild. Fighting down panic, she stilled the tremble in her hands, took the cup in a firm grip, and brought it to her lips. She sniffed the red liquid cautiously. It wasn't blood. The scent of wine rose to her nostrils and she sipped. The warmth in her throat calmed her. She handed the chalice back to the brehon.

Aife raised the chalice high and said in Norse, "You are now husband and wife." Then she made some kind of proclamation in Irish, and the crowd roared in approval.

Murchad took her hand in his. Ragnhild stiffened, but his touch was gentle, his skin warm.

It was done. Relief made her giddy. Murchad's gaze was on her, but she did not meet her husband's eyes.

In a daze, she allowed Murchad to lead her from the hall. The crowd parted before them, shouting well-wishes and strewing flowers at their feet as they crossed the yard to a banquet table. Murchad conducted her to the seat at the head of the table, and the well-wishers gathered around them. He pressed her firmly into the seat beside him while Niall took his place on Murchad's right.

She was queen here, but a prisoner all the same.

A steaming platter of food was set before them. Now that she was in the open air, Ragnhild's stomach rumbled at the scent of fresh bread and roasted meat. The Irish did know how to feast. Her appetite had revived, and she partook in the food and drink with relish.

The Irish skáld rose from his seat, where he was surrounded by his apprentices. They call them bards here, she reminded herself, joining the others in applause. The bard approached Ragnhild and bowed low, speaking in Irish.

Murchad leaned over to her and translated. "The Ollave Seamus presents himself to you, since the patronage of poets falls to the wife. Beware that you do not offend him, for Seamus has a tongue caustic enough to raise blisters and he's brought the mighty to their knees."

Ragnhild smiled at Seamus. She was unlikely to cause offense since they did not share a common language. However, when she met the poet's gaze, she recognized in his eyes a deep comprehension that made her wonder how much Norse the man understood.

Seamus ran his fingers over his harp strings and began to croon in a velvet tone, a lament of some kind that made his listeners sigh. Ragnhild eyed her husband, whose face was rapt, and wondered if all Irishmen were lovesick dupes.

Murchad caught her look and smiled. "The Ollave is telling the story of Grainne and Diarmuid. Grainne was the daughter of the High King of Tara, the most beautiful woman in Ireland." He gave Ragnhild a look that made her fidget. Seamus' melodious voice spoke of longing.

"Grainne had agreed to marry the great hero, Finn Mac Cumhail, but when she saw him at the wedding feast, she was dismayed at how old he was."

"I can understand that," Ragnhild muttered.

Mesmerized by the song, Murchad seemed not to have heard her. "Among the guests was Diarmuid, Finn's strongest and most loyal warrior. Diarmuid had been born with a magic mark on his forehead. Any woman who saw this mark fell in love with him. As you might imagine, this caused all kinds of trouble. Diarmuid wore his hair in such a way that it hid the mark.

"But Grainne's gaze fell on Diarmuid just as he tossed back his head, revealing the magic mark. She fell in love with him.

"Though she had promised to wed Finn, Grainne was a woman who got what she wanted. She sent a sleeping draught to all the men in the room except Diarmuid. But when she demanded that he run away with her, Diarmuid refused. His loyalty to Finn Mac Cumhail was greater than Grainne's attraction, beauty though she was.

"In a fury, Grainne laid a curse on him that forced him to flee with her."

Ragnhild was glad to hear of an Irishwoman taking what she wanted.

Seamus' song became more agitated, the notes fast and chaotic. "Finn pursued the pair, but Diarmuid's foster father, the god Oengus, guided them, advising them never to sleep in the same place twice.

"All the while they were on the run, Diarmuid refused to make love to Grainne, out of loyalty to Finn." Murchad sent her a meaningful look, which she ignored. "But he couldn't resist her forever, and eventually he succumbed.

"Finn pursued them for years, while Grainne gave birth to four sons and a daughter. Finally Oengus managed to negotiate peace between them. The king of Tara gave Finn Grainne's younger sister as a wife, and the old warrior seemed content.

"At last Grainne and Diarmuid were able to settle down and raise their family. They had some happy years. But jealousy ate away at Finn, and the day came when he found Diarmuid wounded in a hunting accident. Though Finn could have saved him, he let his old rival die.

"It is said that Grainne mourned Diarmuid for the rest of her life."

The bard's tones turned mournful as he struck his final note. Everyone in the room fell silent as Seamus bowed before Murchad and Ragnhild.

The silence continued for an uncomfortable amount of time. The bard held his bow for so long, Ragnhild thought his thighs must be crying out from the strain. At last, Murchad cleared his throat and made an announcement in Irish.

The crowd cheered at his words. Seamus straightened up, eyes gleaming in approval as he swept another graceful bow to Ragnhild.

Murchad turned to Ragnhild. "I have just awarded the Ollave ten cows on your behalf, which I will loan you."

Ragnhild's eyebrows shot up.

Murchad grinned at her. "An accomplished Ollave such as Seamus spends twelve years of his life studying. He knows the law, our history, our language. Ten cows is equal to what I paid Aife for our marriage contract. Seamus would be insulted if you gave him less than I gave the brehon, and the satire of an insulted Ollave has been known to topple kings."

While Ragnhild digested this information, Murchad reached into his robe and withdrew a silken pouch. "You are my queen. Now, I will honor you as one." He opened the pouch and brought forth a blaze of gold.

Ragnhild caught her breath. "It is Brisingamen!" she exclaimed. At Murchad's quizzical stare she explained, "The necklace of the goddess Freyja." She stopped short, realizing that in payment Freyja had slept with each of the four dwarves who made it for her.

To her relief, Murchad did not ask for details of the story.

Instead he slid the necklace, made of three golden disks linked by a thick golden chain, over her head.

The metal lay cold and heavy against her skin like slave fetters. She wanted to yank it off, but she controlled her panic. She thought of Åsa, how the queen had bided her time in a forced marriage and gained power. But guile had never been one of Ragnhild's skills. She still cringed at how easily Harald had lured her into this trap. She longed to find her brother and take vengeance. All in good time. First she must deal with this husband.

Murchad said, "This necklace has been worn by the queens of my lineage since ancient times. It is said to give special powers to the one who wears it."

Ragnhild stared at the necklace in a new light—the golden links were power, not fetters. Power she must learn to wield.

There arose a clamoring, a great disturbance at the gate. Murchad looked up as a cluster of guards escorted a crowd of men to them. At their forefront strode a richly dressed man, tall and rangy, with a head of curly, copper-colored hair and a beard to match.

He bowed before Murchad, with a deep nod to Niall, and spoke urgently in Irish, to which Murchad replied.

Murchad turned to Ragnhild, and said in Norse, "My queen, this man is Diarmait, chieftain of the Slaine tribe. We are cousins, but he's recently been allied with my enemy, and so I have asked Diarmait what his business is here."

Diarmait bowed to Ragnhild and murmured some kind of respectful greeting. Ragnhild nodded in return. Then Diarmait straightened and spoke at length. Niall whistled, and Murchad's face split into a broad grin. He clapped the newcomer on the back and gestured expansively for him to join the feast.

One of Murchad's men showed Diarmait to a seat near them, while his retinue found places among the revelers. Murchad clapped his hands, and food and ale were brought to his new guest.

Murchad smiled at Ragnhild. "As my queen, you should know that I seek to overthrow the king of Tara, who styles himself Ard Ri, the High King of all Ireland. My cousin Diarmait has come to join me in this venture." He paused to gauge her reaction.

Ragnhild bared her teeth in a grin. This sounded interesting. "Who is this High King, and why do you seek to overthrow him?"

"Conchobar mac Donnchada is a treacherous bastard," said Murchad, his color rising. "He's king of the southern branch of my family, the Ui Neill. He claims the title of High King of all Ireland. But I should be the Ard Ri." At the words Ard Ri, Diarmait raised his cup to Murchad, who inclined his head and continued in Norse, "Niall's father, Aed, was the last Ard Ri, and he raised us both to be kings." He turned back to Diarmait, and soon they were deep in discussion.

Ragnhild eyed Niall, who sat listening to Diarmait and Murchad. She wondered how Niall felt about Murchad holding the kingship. Surely as the king's son Niall had the better claim?

As the summer sky deepened into evening, pipers played their strange, sweet music that raised a wildness in her breast. When the food was demolished and the bard made his final bow, Murchad took her hand, startling her back to the present.

"The hour grows late, my queen."

Ragnhild's stomach knotted. Would he keep his word? Murchad stood and offered her his arm. Ragnhild rose and laid her hand on his. In her other hand she clutched her eating knife, reassured to have a weapon of sorts. She stepped down from the high seat and allowed him to lead her to the doorway of the hall. The merrymakers crowded behind with hoots and howls, shoving them through the dark opening.

Inside, Murchad slammed the oak door on them and turned to her, breathless and cheerful. He smiled at her. "You look lovely, wife."

Ragnhild ignored that, gripping her eating knife low at her side. Perhaps she would still take vengeance for her father's death.

Murchad poured a cup of mead and handed it to her. "We might as well make this evening pleasant." His gaze went to the knife in her hand. "There's no need for that."

"A marriage in name only," she reminded him.

Murchad smiled, holding his hands out wide. "We can at least toast each other with the bridal mead. T'would be a shame to waste it."

Ragnhild kept a firm grip on the knife as she accepted the cup from his hand and sniffed it suspiciously. The scent of honey mead rose in her nostrils.

"I gave you my word that nothing would happen that you did not want," said Murchad.

"I am your prisoner. That is not my will."

"I cannot let you go. To do so would endanger my people. You must remain by my side, to ensure the treaty remains in effect. I cannot have your brother attack my people as your father did."

"In other words, I am a hostage to ensure my brother's behavior," she retorted.

"You are no hostage. You are my queen, and I will honor you as such. And don't forget, it was your own father who arranged our marriage."

"I fought a war against my father to keep from being sold to you as a peace-cow." Ragnhild stared into her cup morosely. "In the end, he lost to you, and so have I."

Murchad smiled at her. "You fought a war so that you wouldn't have to marry me? You are like the Irish queens of ancient times, who made war and led men into battle."

Ragnhild said nothing, though the admiration in his voice made her flush. She raised the cup and sipped. The mead soothed her throat and warmed her stomach.

"I never knew my father," said Murchad. "He was killed the

same year I was born by our enemies, the Conaills. My mother died soon after of a broken heart and I was taken in by Niall's father. He was king of Aileach before me, and also Ard Ri. He trained me to be a Christian, a warrior, a poet, a king. But the Conaills murdered him, too. I avenged his death, and the people of the North elected me to be king of Aileach."

So that was why Niall was not king. It was Murchad who had taken vengeance.

"I should have become Ard Ri as well. But while I was fighting the Conaills, the bastard Conchobar mac Donnchada stole the title. I raised an army to claim what should be mine. Conchobar and I met on the battlefield three years ago, but the men of Ulaid were with him, making our forces evenly matched. So we withdrew."

"You withdrew when you were evenly matched?" Ragnhild exclaimed, incredulous. "What kind of white-livered cowards are you?"

"Ah, *a chroí*, we Irish only fight when we are sure to win." He raised his glass to his uncomprehending guest. "But now Diarmait and the men of Brega have decided to join my cause, and victory will be mine."

"What makes you sure that Conchobar won't run away when he sees he's outnumbered?"

Murchad smiled broadly. "Because the bastard won't know he's outnumbered until it's too late."

"So Diarmait will seem to be with him, then change sides during the battle?"

"Exactly! What a clever wife I've married!"

"How can you be sure Diarmait will keep his end of the bargain?"

Murchad eyed his guest speculatively. "Because, *a mhuirín*, I will have a man on either side of him with their knives drawn."

So, the Irish trust each other no more than the Norse do. She sipped her mead, eyeing her husband. He was a clever man. She would have to watch her step with him.

Murchad cleared his throat and looked at her over the rim of his cup. "Father Ferdia still wants to baptize you. He objects to a king of the Cenel nEoghan wedding a heathen bride. As does my cousin."

Ragnhild stiffened. "I told you I will never become a Christian. I could never worship a god who let his enemies nail him to a tree without killing a single one. And your minor gods are worse, each one more cowardly than the last."

Murchad quaffed his mead. "We call them saints. And it's a little more complicated than that." He gave her a mischievous smile. "The best thing about being a Christian is that I don't have to cover a mare every year to be king."

Ragnhild choked on her mead, nearly spewing it on the silk gown.

"It's true!" He stifled a laugh. "When the Irish were yet heathen, the king had to mount a mare, and complete the act in front of a crowd, no less. I'm very happy the priests declared that duty blasphemy."

The picture that formed in her mind was too much. Ragnhild tried to keep a stone face but a snort escaped her. Murchad sniggered and she exploded into laughter. "Our kings don't have to do anything like that!"

"I doubt if any Norseman would be up to it," he said, making her laugh even harder. "It was a very solemn ceremony," he admonished. They both howled in helpless mirth, falling on the bed.

At last, gasping, they stopped for breath. His eyes met hers and held them.

He reached out one finger and traced a line down her tattoo. His hand slid behind her neck and he drew her face toward his.

His eyes were closed, his lips parted. A shiver ran up Ragnhild's spine. Her belly was warm, liquid, and she wanted him to touch her. A lassitude came over her, a passiveness.

Weakness.

She jerked away. "This is not our bargain!"

His eyes flew open. "I'm sorry."

Ragnhild scrambled off the bed and made for the door.

He was on his feet and blocked her way. "Stay, please."

She kept her head lowered, staring at the door.

"I won't touch you again." He bowed and left by the side door, taking his mead cup with him.

She stared after her husband and wondered how to handle him.

CHAPTER 10

Lough Feabhail

"Ship your oars and draw your bows!" cried Einar, watching *Battle Swan* and *Wave Steed* close in on either side to catch *Raider Bride* between them, the scout's karvi blocking the harbor entrance, cutting off retreat. The two attacking ships were much longer than *Raider Bride* and between them outnumbered *Raider Bride's* crew by more than double.

Raider Bride's crew stood back to back, facing the oncoming ships.

"Nock!" Einar shouted. The crew fitted their arrows. "Draw!" The bows creaked. The attackers had the choice to have their oarsmen take cover or keep coming.

They kept coming.

The first volley had to count.

Einar waited until the enemy ships were close enough that he could read the triumph in Harald's eyes.

"Loose!"

Arrows whickered across the water from both sides of *Raider Bride*, finding their mark in an enemy with enough force to pierce chain mail. Screams echoed and men thudded onto the deck.

The volley thinned the enemy ranks, but still they came.

The two enemy ships hove alongside. Grappling hooks sailed across, thumping onto *Raider Bride's* sheer strake between the shields. The attackers shipped oars and took up spears and axes. But to board they had to climb across a barrier of fallen shipmates as well as the row of shields racked on *Raider Bride's* rail.

It gave Einar time for one more volley.

"Nock!" he shouted. The enemy raised their shields. "Draw! Loose!"

Fired at point-blank range, the onslaught shattered the wooden shields and gouged big gaps in the front lines of each ship. Screams filled the air while gulls began to circle.

Einar liked the odds better now. *Raider Bride's* crew cast aside their bows to grab spears and axes, eyes on the enemy. The boarders hesitated.

"Kill them, you sorry bastards, or I'll split you in half!" Harald screamed, hefting his axe and kicking a corpse aside. His crew heaved the dead overboard and crowded to the rail.

With both hands Einar swung his axe into an enemy neck, taking the man's head half off. The Orcadian went down in a geyser of blood. Beside him Unn faced a much taller opponent. She rammed her spear up under his chin, checking the swing of his sword. She yanked the spear from his throat, and a gurgling spray of blood drenched her. Without missing a beat she thrust at the next man in line, but he pivoted and Unn's spearhead glanced off his mail, leaving her wide open to his axe swing.

"Watch out!" Einar cried as he knocked the axe away with his own. Unn recovered and drove her spear into the enemy's throat.

Men roared in fury and screamed in pain. Gulls shrieked, wheeling above the blood-slicked decks, ready to dive into the gore. From the corner of his eye Einar glimpsed Svein and Thorgeir in the stern, axes flailing into a mob of attackers.

He had to get *Raider Bride* free before they were boarded. He swept his own axe across the grappling hook rope, parting it one stroke, but they stuck fast between the enemy ships.

Einar glanced aft. Harald fought in the stern of the *Swan*, roaring as he hacked his sword at Svein, who fended him off coolly with his axe.

A blade flashed and Einar ducked behind a shield racked on the rail. Splinters shot into the air but the axe blade stuck in the wood. Einar grabbed his assailant's shield and yanked him off his feet while Unn spitted him. The decks of *Battle Swan* were packed with bodies, leaving little fighting room to those still on their feet. With minimal casualties, *Raider Bride's* crew had improved the odds dramatically.

"Gut the bastards!" Einar bellowed, and the crew swarmed forward, blades flashing.

"Cut the lines!" Harald cried. His men chopped their own ropes in a frantic effort to escape the onslaught.

The enemy ships fell away, and their diminished crews ran out their oars and stroked hard toward the karvi waiting at the entrance. Once clear of the cove, all three ships loosed their sails and disappeared around the headland.

"Harald never did like a fair fight," observed Svein.

Einar counted the bodies in the water and guessed at the number he'd seen on the enemy decks. "They still outnumber us. When Harald realizes it, he'll be back."

"You're right," said Thorgeir. "We'd better get away ourselves as soon as they're out of sight."

Einar surveyed the damage to the crew. He recognized four farm boys he had trained, bobbing among the corpses in the water. There were plenty of minor wounds and a few broken bones. Gore-spattered but apparently unhurt, Unn bandaged an axe cut on a farm boy's leg. A shield-maiden huddled over a spear that had penetrated her gut. She moaned softly as Svein drew the spearhead out. He patted her and said, "There, it's out now." Thorgeir moved in with a bandage to staunch the blood.

Once the wounded were stabilized, Thorgeir and Svein came forward, breathing hard and covered with blood that was not their own. They manned the oars and waited while others did the same.

Einar took his place at the tiller and barked, "Row!"

Raider Bride moved away from the carnage.

BEHRT SWAM slowly up to consciousness. He kept his eyes closed against the sun's assault, making a mental assessment of his body before he stirred. There was no part of him that did not hurt. His head throbbed, his back ached, his shoulders fairly screamed. Even breathing caused him pain.

"You must drink this," came a gentle voice.

Behrt opened his eyes, steeling himself against the jolt that shot through his head. Sunlight lanced through a wall of woven withies. Earnest gray eyes peered at him from a sun-darkened, brown-bearded face. The man held an earthenware cup to Behrt's lips. "Come, drink," the man urged.

The scent of herbs rose from the steaming cup. Behrt opened his lips gingerly. A spear of pain shot from his jaw. He sipped the hot liquid.

"That's it. That's it." The wild-bearded man patted his shoulder gently. "You'll do fine, now."

Behrt could not quite summon the strength to speak. He glanced around, careful not to move his head. He was in some sort of woodland shelter, lying on a heather pallet.

"I found you nearly dead," said his host. "Someone—a number of someones—had beaten you soundly. You are lucky I came upon you when I did, for you would have died for sure if you'd lain there much longer. Ethne and I got you back here." The man gestured toward a doe, whose head poked in the opening of the shelter. Ethne regarded him, concern gleaming in her large, brown eyes. "I'm Brother Brian," her master added hurriedly.

For the first time Behrt noticed that his savior wore a threadbare brown robe, and his head was tonsured in front.

"Where am I, Brother?" said Behrt. His voice was a croak. The small shelter, barely big enough for the two of them, appeared to be constructed of branches, intricately woven and thatched with bracken. Dappled sunlight shone through the walls and in the open doorway, where Ethne the doe nibbled on some leaves that seemed to be growing from the doorframe.

"You are at my home," said Brother Brian. "My hermit's cell, deep in the forest. You are safe. No one comes here."

Behrt had heard of such hermit monks, those who took the path of green martyrdom and went into exile for Jesus, leading lives of hardship, fasting, and prayer, but he'd never met one before. Often there was a reason for them to seek solitude. He wondered if Brother Brian had a shadowed past.

"Your injuries are severe, but you should recover," the hermit continued. "I can treat you here, until you are able to travel."

"I am most grateful, Brother. I don't wish to impose on your hospitality."

"It's no imposition at all. It is my privilege to serve."

Behrt's shoulders relaxed. He'd been tensing himself in preparation for…crawling away to die in the forest, apparently.

"You have been sorely injured in the past," Brother Brian said. "Your body bears many scars."

Behrt winced as the monk gently probed his ribs. "Yes, I am… was…a warrior." He realized that he wore nothing but his tunic and breeks. His sword, knife, battle-jacket, even his boots were gone. He looked around the hut, but it was bare except for bundles of herbs hanging from the ceiling, a few pieces of crockery lined up against the walls, and a curious squirrel who stared at him before scurrying out through the branches.

"This is how I found you," said Brother Brian.

So the Irishmen had beaten him, robbed him, and left him for dead.

Welcome home.

CHAPTER 11

Aileach Cashel

Ragnhild woke alone in Murchad's bed. On the floor lay the silk leine she'd been married in, and she lay naked beneath linen sheets.

Fiona emerged from a corner where she'd been lurking. The Irishwoman came forward with tunic and breeks, muttering in a scolding tone. While Ragnhild pulled on her clothes, Fiona carefully folded the silk dress, then took Ragnhild firmly by the arm and conducted her back to the women's quarters.

The Irishwomen perched on their alcoves, spinning flax while they prattled in their language. They cast dark looks in Ragnhild's direction with mutters of *finn gaill,* the same word Fiona had scolded her with, a term that apparently referred to her, and not in a complimentary way.

Ragnhild ignored them and settled in her alcove. Her nose alerted her to the pot that bubbled over the fire.

"*Leite,*" Fiona said as she handed her a bowl filled with

steaming oats. Ragnhild accepted the bowl and wolfed down the porridge, ignoring her burned tongue.

Murchad appeared in the doorway. He spoke to Fiona, and the Irishwoman rose and packed the silk dress carefully in an oak chest. She bustled about the room, picking up other items and stowing them in the chest.

"We must make ready to depart," Murchad said to Ragnhild. "We must reach the Grianan before evening."

Ragnhild's heart beat harder. She didn't know where the Grianan was, but leaving this fortress presented another opportunity to escape.

Brunaidh waited outside the walls with the other horses. Murchad nodded and the boy led the pony to a mounting block. Ragnhild felt herself blush, but for Brunaidh's sake she stepped onto the block, promising herself she would soon learn to spring onto a horse's back as gracefully as Murchad himself.

The party set off through the gates, Murchad keeping close to Ragnhild, his warriors once again hemming her in. Niall rode with them, as did Diarmait and his men. Nearly every person in the fortress followed, on horseback or on foot, leaving behind a handful of warriors to guard the walls.

Brunaidh was sure-footed with an easy gait. It was a fine morning for a ride—but every step took Ragnhild farther from *Raider Bride*. She gazed back over her shoulder at the now-distant river, a heaviness settling in her chest.

They followed a narrow causeway of logs and stone that crossed a strip of marshland to the north and west. The ground firmed beneath the horses' hooves as they skirted a hill that rose high above the broad valley surrounding them. The hill was an island in a sea of marshland. Even if Ragnhild could break free she dare not depart from the narrow trail. Her captors would ride her down with ease. She would have to bide her time and wait for a better opportunity.

Another hill rose in the distance, nearly as tall as the one they rounded and crowned by a ringfort.

"That is Greenan Mountain." Murchad gestured toward the hilltop, pride in his voice. "On the crest stands the Grianan, the palace of the sun. My father won this mountain and the surrounding lands from the Conaills before I was born. It has been a coronation site since ancient times, and now it is ours."

By late afternoon they had crossed the marshy valley and mounted the base of the hill. They started up a gradual, rocky trail cut through the heather. Near the top, they rode through a series of three concentric earthen berms that encircled the hilltop. The berms had been eroded over time so they were no more than rounded humps, and heather grew thick on their rounded tops.

"These outer ramparts are ancient," said Murchad. "Legends say the original ringfort was built by the Dagda, lord of the Tuatha de Danaan, the ancient people of Ireland. Some say they were gods. They say the Dagda's son, Aed, lies buried in that tomb." He gestured at a mound on the south flank of the hill. It was surrounded by ten man-sized stones that lay flat in a circle, radiating out from the mound like the rays of the sun.

"The Tuatha de Danaan were driven underground, long ago," he continued. "There are those who believe they dwell beneath us, within this hill, to this day." Ragnhild shivered. She could feel the power of this place.

As they passed through the innermost berm, the formidable stone wall of the fortress confronted them. Murchad dismounted and lifted Ragnhild from Brunaidh's back. The boy appeared and took the pony's bridle, leading her off to a corral built of withy stakes. A jolt of fear shot through Ragnhild as she watched her only friend walk away.

"Wait," she called. She shook off Murchad's hold and hurried over to the boy, who stood as if frozen. She stared at him, realizing she didn't even know how to ask his name. She glowered at

Murchad. She must rely on him for everything. "What is his name?"

With a smile, Murchad translated.

The boy answered in a nervous chirp. "Fergal." He ducked his head respectfully.

"Fergal," Ragnhild repeated. He nodded. Knowing his name made it somehow easier to let him lead Brunaidh away. She gestured for him to continue.

Murchad put a hand on her shoulder and gently propelled her forward. The road narrowed and curved to the right, lined by an avenue of stone. From the top of the wall, men watched their approach. "This is a ceremonial place," said Murchad. "Normally, we keep only a small garrison here as lookouts. But now the folk are gathering for the solstice."

The road circled the wall until it ended at a low, narrow oak doorway set into the east side. The door creaked open and Ragnhild tensed. Murchad gripped her elbow and pushed her into the low, dark entry. The people crowded in behind. A chill passed over Ragnhild as she crouched almost double to enter the passage through the wall, but this time she was ready. She hobbled through, gaze fixed on the daylight ahead.

The passage opened on a broad yard scattered with a few round, thatched shelters of varying sizes. There were no squawking chickens this time. In the center of the yard stood a raised, flat-topped stone the length and height of a man.

Murchad was engaged in greetings with one of the guard. Ragnhild took a breath and examined the fortifications.

The wall was comprised of three concentric stone terraces of ascending height that could be mounted by flights of stone steps. Ragnhild glanced at Murchad. He was still deep in discussion, so she strode to the nearest steps and climbed onto the wall.

The men on the wall watched her, but they did not approach. She was their queen, after all. Before her, a short run of stairs led to the next terrace where the watch stood. She took the steps in a few strides.

She peered out over the outer wall and caught her breath. The country spread out before her like a map, revealing the twisting ribbon of river they'd come in on, the vast inlet beyond—the Lough Feabhail. To the west, another immense body of water reached across the land. Beyond it all, the sea itself glinted like a sheet of silver beneath the low sun.

This view was a gift from the gods. Turning slowly, Ragnhild studied the lay of the land carefully, marking the course of the many rivers and waterways, and sprawling boglands punctuated by hills. Her gaze followed the black form of a crow as it winged across the land toward the sea. A lump formed in her throat. Where was *Raider Bride*? How would she ever find her ship?

"It's a magical view." Murchad had come up silently behind her.

The lump in Ragnhild's throat blocked her words. She could only nod her head.

"My people lay claim to all the land as far as you can see."

Ragnhild glanced up at the Irish king as he gazed out over the land, his expression rapt. She could almost read his thoughts.

Murchad turned to face the center of the fortress, sweeping his arm toward the enormous flat stone that stood in the yard. "On that rock, I received my kingship. Kings have been anointed here since ancient times." From her vantage point above it, Ragnhild could make out what looked like two footprints carved in the top of the stone.

As the sun neared the horizon, Murchad said, "Come, our people are waiting. We must preside over the sacred fire. Tonight we celebrate the solstice."

Shock gave Ragnhild her voice. "I thought Christ-followers did not believe in such things."

Murchad gave her a strange smile and turned his gaze to the setting sun. "The old ones are still here, in every valley and grove.

Only a fool neglects them. Saint John's Eve conveniently coincides with the solstice."

He took her hand and led her along the wall to the western side. Two chairs had been set up beside a brazier, next to a small table with cups of mead. Beneath the wall, a crowd had gathered. As Ragnhild and Murchad appeared, people looked up and cheered.

Murchad accepted a flaming branch from one of his men and waited, watching the sun. As the glowing ball slipped below the horizon, he touched the branch to the kindling in the brazier. The fire caught just as the sun winked out into the sea. As the blaze flared up, points of light bloomed across the darkening countryside while onlookers lit their own bonfires below the walls.

Sparks flew into the deepening colors of the sky while below, pipes played a haunting melody. Voices joined in. People rose and began to dance. Couples leaped through the flames, holding hands.

"To ensure a good harvest," Murchad said.

This was not so very different than midsummer at home. Ragnhild relaxed and began to enjoy the evening. She and Murchad sat sipping mead while the music and fire leaping continued. Far below, lights moved down the hillside.

Murchad nodded at the lights. "The farmers carry torches through the fields in tribute to the sun goddess, Aine, who protects the crops and the cattle. She's the goddess of summer, and of love. If you ever see a red mare, so fast that no one can outrun her, that's Aine, come to walk among her people. There is a tale that a mighty king raped her, but in revenge Aine bit off his ear, rendering him unfit to be king, for in this land, a king must be whole and sound of body."

The more she heard about this goddess, the more Ragnhild liked her. She sounded a bit like Freyja. Perhaps Irishwomen had not always been such snivelers as Fiona and her ilk.

Ollave Seamus approached and bowed before them. He strummed his harp and his rich voice resonated in a magical song. Murchad listened for a moment, head thrown back, eyes closed, then began to speak. "He's singing the tale of Aileach, the daughter of a Scottish king. Frigrind was a Pictish builder who fell in love with her, and she with him. But the Scottish king would not allow his daughter to marry a craftsman. Aileach and Frigrind fled here, to Ireland, and the king gave them this ancient fortress for a sanctuary. Frigrind built a house from red yew, carved and inlaid with gold and jewels."

The bard's lilting voice held Ragnhild captive as she watched the stars and the moon glimmer on the distant sea. The enchantment of this land came over her.

Ollave Seamus fell silent and another voice rose from below—still sweet, but lighter, less resonant. "One of his apprentices," explained Murchad.

The bard had twenty-four apprentices, and each of them took a turn that night, continuing the songs until dawn. Murchad translated each story to her as they sipped mead and watched the fire.

At last the horizon began to glow. Ragnhild watched in silent awe as the sun burst up over the sea, casting its light across the water, and Ollave Seamus strummed his harp and sang in praise of the dawn. As the bard's final notes resonated, people began to depart, each carrying a firebrand.

"They light their hearth fires with a brand from the solstice fires," said Murchad.

They watched the light change until the sun was fully risen. When the last person departed, Murchad rose and held out his hand to Ragnhild. She took it and followed him down the steps.

In the yard, breakfast porridge bubbled over the fire. Sleepy folk sat on benches, calling their blessings on their king and his new queen. They took the high seat and Fiona served them steaming bowls.

~

EINAR GUIDED *Raider Bride* into the shallows at the extreme northern end of the Lough, close to the sea and far from the place they had been separated from Ragnhild. He had them bring the longship among the reeds to rest and tend the wounded.

He took stock of their situation. Of *Raider Bride's* thirty-six original crewmembers, four had been killed in the battle and their bodies left behind. Six more were wounded, and two of them looked certain to die. Ragnhild and the Christian were still missing.

One lad was raving with a festering leg wound that would kill him soon enough, despite Unn's best efforts to keep it clean. The other seriously wounded warrior was the farm girl who had taken a spear to her gut. She lay in the bow on a pile of furs, gray-faced and silent.

The other four wounded had injuries that did not appear to be life-threatening, at least for now. Einar knew how quickly that could change, especially living rough as they were. Einar had popped one boy's dislocated shoulder back into place, but the arm hung uselessly in a sling while the injury healed. Einar knew from past experience that the boy would not be fighting or rowing for several weeks. The other injuries consisted of a swordblow to the head, accompanied by disabling headaches that came and went, a lacerated arm, and a nasty but clean gash in the thigh. Given time and rest, these four would most likely mend.

But time was in short supply.

Einar conferred with the crew, trying to chart a course of action. "It appears Harald and Kol have left the area. I hope they are headed home. I don't know where the Christian is." He shrugged. "This is his country. He could be anywhere. And Ragnhild is prisoner of the Irish king."

"The same man King Solvi had promised her to in an alliance

between the two kingdoms," said Svein. "Presumably the Irishman had made the same arrangement with Harald."

"Clever of Harald, swindling his sister out of her inheritance in exchange for a hefty chest of treasure," Thorgeir observed. "That boy was always out for himself alone."

Einar considered. "If that is true, then the Irish king needs Ragnhild alive for the alliance to be valid. She's a prisoner, but probably not in danger."

"Unless she tries to escape, which of course she will," said Thorgeir.

Einar raked his fingers through his hair and paced the deck. Indecision knotted his guts and he ground his teeth. "We don't know where the Irish have taken Ragnhild. What can we do with our small numbers? Should we search for her or return to Tromøy and seek help?"

"Ragnhild wouldn't abandon any one of us," said Unn.

"She's right," said Thorgeir. "We can't leave her behind."

"But if we search for Ragnhild, we might never find her, and we risk an encounter with the Irish," said Svein. "Even if we find someone who speaks Norse, and is willing to give us information rather than the edge of their sword. If we return to Tromøy, Åsa and Heid might be able to locate Ragnhild with their powers, and send a larger rescue party."

"There are risks in going home," Einar pointed out. "The trip would take two weeks or more, and we're short-crewed. We'll have to pass between the Southern Isles and through the Orkneys, and sail too close to Solbakk for comfort. Once we reach Tromøy and muster a war party, it would take at least two more weeks to get back to Ireland. Ragnhild won't endure captivity peacefully for a month. Anything could happen."

Unn turned the discussion from the dilemma to the practical. "This will take some thought. In the meantime, we have to eat." She doled out a cold meal of dried meat and flatbread.

Filled with foreboding, Einar assigned watches for the night.

He wrapped himself in damp furs and fell into an uneasy sleep. The wounded boy's ravings entered his dreams, and he woke every hour or so to glimpse the moon as it lurked among the clouds.

Just before dawn, the boy ceased his raving. The abrupt silence woke Einar from a fraught doze. He struggled out of his sheepskin, though he knew there was nothing he could do. Unn was already by the lad's side.

"He's dead," she said. "So is Hild." The girl had slipped away without a sound. Einar's gut felt hollow, as if he'd been punched.

In the chill dawn, the crew committed the dead to the sea goddess, Ran, mumbling a prayer that she'd welcome them in her hall beneath the waves. Einar wished he could bury them properly in a mound with the rituals they deserved, but in this hostile land, that risked discovery and capture. They had died fighting, and that should earn them an honored place in the kingdom of the dead. Should he survive to return to Tromøy, he would commission a rune stone carved to honor them.

They heaved the bodies overboard. As the current caught the corpses and carried them downstream, Einar's spirit seemed to follow them.

He dragged his gaze from the departed as Unn rationed out breakfast. While the crew gnawed their flatbread and dried meat, he pondered what action they could take. The futility of it weighed in his chest like wet wool.

"We don't have enough food or water to make the passage home," Unn pointed out. "We'll have to spend at least a day fishing and find a spring to fill the waterskins, then another day to preserve the fish. There's no time to dry the fish, so we'll have to risk a low fire at night to smoke them."

With relief, Einar realized they could postpone the decision while they reprovisioned.

He decided to risk keeping the mast up. They were in decent cover right now, though the spar stuck up above the trees about three feet. Lowering the mast was a daunting task, requiring the entire crew. There was a real risk of dropping the spar, causing damage to the hull and the mast itself, possibly injuring crewmembers, and before they could venture out into the open sea they'd have to raise it again, an even more perilous task.

They'd just have to trust to luck and hope the Irish were not too observant.

He assigned crewmembers to fish while Unn and Thorgeir led a shore party with the waterskins and sacks for anything edible they may find in the countryside. Einar stayed aboard to supervise the fishing party and tend the wounded.

Once they had enough food laid in, the decision would have to be made whether to flee for home or try to find Ragnhild. No matter what they decided, Einar worried about running into Harald again. They had been lucky the last time, with the element of surprise. In another encounter things might not be in their favor.

The fishermen pulled aboard several fat salmon and brown trout. Einar helped them clean the fish and fillet them into thin slices that would cure quickly. As evening fell, he sent Svein and a helper ashore with their hudfat. They built a low fire and set the thin slices of fish on rocks downwind of the fire to cure in the smoke overnight. They also cooked a few whole fish directly over the fire to eat that night.

The shore party straggled back just before dark with full waterskins and sacks crammed with edible plants that Unn had identified. Svein sent several of the cooked fish aboard with them.

The hot meal cheered the crew, and they chatted quietly together until a chill rain began to fall, driving them to the relative comfort of their hudfat.

Einar burrowed into his fleece and curled up so that only his nose was exposed to the cold air. He wished he dared raise their awning, but it was too conspicuous and would encumber them if they needed to get away fast. He listened to the rain pattering on the deck and fell asleep wondering what to do.

At dawn, Svein and his helper were returning with the smoked fish when one of the local fishing boats passed by their hiding place. The Irish crew must have spotted *Raider Bride's* mast sticking up among the trees, for they gave a shout and pulled up short. The foliage parted and the Irishmen gaped at the Norse, then spun their craft around and paddled away.

"After them," Einar shouted.

The crew leaped to their oars and thrashed their way out of the creek, but by the time they made it out of their hiding spot, the Irish boat had threaded its way into a watercourse riddled with sandbars. Einar surveyed the convoluted shallows. The channel appeared to be marked by withy stakes, but if *Raider Bride* went aground here, they would be helpless.

"Halt!" he called. The oarsmen backed water and hung in the current.

"They'll return with reinforcements," said Thorgeir.

Einar nodded grimly. "We need to get out of here." He set them on a downstream course toward open water. They heaved on the oars, sending the longship skimming over the water, outrunning the current. They overtook their fallen comrades, rowing past the corpses in grim silence.

It was their bad luck that reinforcements were very close indeed. A fleet of the flimsy craft swarmed out of the waterway, crammed with Irish warriors screaming war cries and brandishing spears.

Flimsy they might have been, but there were a lot of them, and they were light and fast.

"Row!" shouted Einar.

Though the longship was inherently faster than the Irish craft, with the wounded unable to row, the remaining crew of *Raider Bride* were hard put to keep ahead of the enemy fleet. Soon the currachs closed in around them.

"Ram them," Einar ordered, hoping they could break through to clear water beyond. The rowers gave their oars a mighty thrust. *Raider Bride's* oak prow slammed into the lead boat, crushing the fragile craft, but the wreckage caught on the prow, stopping the longship dead in the water. The displaced Irish crew leaped aboard other boats that surged alongside in a flurry of grappling hooks, ensnaring *Raider Bride* in a web of braided line.

"Ship oars," Einar bellowed, abandoning the tiller and hefting his axe. As their captors cinched in the lines, *Raider Bride's* crew drew weapons and hacked at the ropes in a futile attempt to break free.

The Irish commander shouted an order and Einar's spine prickled. He didn't have to speak the language to understand the tone.

"Shield fort!" Einar cried. The crew flung their shields overhead just as a hail of spears and arrows thwacked down on *Raider Bride*. The shields overhead formed a roof while others created a side wall. The Norse thrust their spear points between the shields.

The Irish trained a thicket of spears on the Norse, holding them at bay behind their shield fort. Einar peered out between the gaps, seeking a chance to turn the situation in his favor. What he saw made his stomach churn. *Raider Bride* was effectively caught in a mass of enemy craft. If the Irish rushed the shield fort, they would die on the Norse spears thrust between the shields. It was a standoff, at least as long as *Raider Bride's* crew could hold the shield wall. Their captors could simply wait them out, then move in for the slaughter. He had to figure a way to survive this.

At a barked order, the Irish crews ran out their oars and began to row, propelling the entire flotilla up the waterway, *Raider Bride* ensnared in their midst. Their craft were not as awkward as they looked, and the Irishmen maneuvered with efficient skill.

The Irish brought the flotilla alongside a rickety dock and made fast. From between the shields Einar glimpsed more warriors thronging the shore. He tried to estimate their numbers, but all he could tell for certain was that his crew was vastly outnumbered.

"I'm going out there," he said.

"They'll slaughter you," said Thorgeir.

Einar shrugged. He couldn't see any other way.

He laid down his spear and, gripping his shield with both hands, raised it up and down above his head, hoping the Irish understood the traditional sign of parlay.

He waited a heartbeat, then shoved his way out of the shield fort. He stood motionless, holding the shield high above his head, his body a perfect target.

There was plenty of shouting but nobody came near. Einar held his position, arms beginning to ache.

At last one of the warriors broke free and approached him. Einar firmed the tremble out of his arms and made a stone face. The Irishman was as tall and lean as the spear he carried. He wore no armor, just a linen robe belted at the waist and a woolen cloak caught at his shoulder by a silver pin.

"Greetings," said the Irishman in heavily accented Norse. "I am called Aed. I know a little of your language. You may speak to me."

Einar lowered his shield.

"If you and your crew surrender, we will do you no harm," said Aed, nodding to the barbed shield fort.

Einar didn't trust the man, but he had little choice. They couldn't maintain their defensive position indefinitely. He turned to the others, clustered behind their shields.

"He says if we surrender, they won't harm us. We can lay down our arms, or fight," he said. "It's your choice."

"If we fight, we will all certainly die," said Unn. "If we surrender, we may find a way to escape."

"The girl speaks sense," said Thorgeir.

"But if we fight and die, we will be sure to go to Valhöll," said Svein. "As outnumbered as we are, it will be over quickly. If we let these Irish pigs take us captive, we'll likely die a slow death of sickness or starvation. Then we will end up in Helheim."

The goddess Hel's icy realm was not an appealing thought.

"It's easy for us battle-worn veterans to give up our lives," said Thorgeir. "It's quite another to sentence these youngsters to death."

"It's hard to argue with that," said Svein. "I am willing to surrender for the sake of our young crewmembers, with the goal of escape."

"Do you all agree?" said Einar. From the shield fort came murmurs of assent and no nays. "Very well, put down your shields."

The crew of *Raider Bride* lowered their shields, peering out at their captors.

"Tell them to lay down their weapons," said Aed, crossing his arms over his chest.

Once the crew had laid their axes and spears atop their shields on *Raider Bride's* deck, Aed motioned them onto the pier. Supporting the wounded, they stepped off the boat and gathered around Einar. Irish warriors came forward to bind their hands and loop a long rope made up of nooses around their necks, forming them into a slave chain. The injured were roped alongside healthy crewmembers who helped them stumble along. Einar was relieved they weren't using chains—until he discovered that the nooses were tied with slip-knots, and if the prisoners didn't keep up, the rope would tighten around their throats.

Einar's heart hit bottom as their captors prodded the crew with spears and hauled on the rope, dragging them to captivity. Immediate death might have been a better choice than the slow one of slavery—but he still harbored hopes of escape.

The Irishmen marched *Raider Bride's* crew toward a fortress, its timber palisade mounted on a rock base. The Irish drove the captives through a gate straddled by a wooden watchtower. Inside, warriors stared down at them from an elevated walkway that ran around the palisade. Einar noted that it was accessed by a single ladder.

The yard housed a dozen or more round, thatched structures of varying size. Women and children went about their chores among flocks of chickens and geese. Einar craned his neck to take in the fortress while their captors herded them to a hovel and shoved the whole chain of them through the door. As he tumbled in with the others, Einar heard the clunk of the latch.

Daylight filtered through the withy walls, casting dim light on a dank prison that by the smell had recently housed cattle.

"What are they going to do with us?" asked Unn, her gaze darting around the byre.

"They probably don't know themselves," said Thorgeir. "They may have to consult a higher authority than the man we surrendered to."

"Untie each other, and look to the wounded," said Einar to distract them from their plight. Best to keep busy.

The knots of their bonds had drawn tight during the forced march, and without knives it took some time to free themselves. There was no water or bedding, so they made the wounded as comfortable as they could on the packed-earth floor.

"Get some rest while you can," said Einar. He lowered himself to the floor, leaned his head against the wattle wall and closed his eyes.

CHAPTER 12

Greenan Mountain

Two more enchanted days passed at the Grianan. Ragnhild spent her time outside, reveling in the long summer days. In the evenings she watched the sunset from the top of the wall, Murchad beside her. She slept bundled in a sheepskin under the stars, snug against the night mist that blew in from the sea, while the bards sang them to sleep. Murchad lay next to her, chastely wrapped in his own sheepskin, murmuring translations, and the stories followed Ragnhild into her dreams.

Murchad spent his days in council with his men, leaving Ragnhild to pace the walls, memorizing the lay of the land, the location of the rare causeways and tracks that crossed the moors, the curve of the rivers, the spread of the oak forests. She spent much of her time in the corral with Brunaidh, grooming the pony, practicing leaping onto her back, and talking to her. The pony's ears twitched in a friendly way that said she understood everything Ragnhild said to her.

Fiona and the other women followed her everywhere, incessantly trying to teach her the language. Though Ragnhild pretended to pay no attention, she listened carefully, striving to attach words to objects. Between their chatter and the evening songs, Ragnhild began to pick up a word here and there.

Murchad announced that they would be leaving again. "It is time to return to our ancestral home," he said. "The place I inherited from my father, the home that belongs to us alone."

Ragnhild was ready to get out of this fortress. For all its grandeur, it was too well guarded. Another journey was another chance to escape, this time with a mental map in her head.

On the morning of their departure, they walked through the low entrance. Outside the walls, Fiona and the other women clustered, calling out orders to men who were loading food and baggage onto pack horses.

Fergal stood among the boys, holding Brunaidh ready. Ragnhild approached the pony with her jaw set. She gripped the single rein, took a deep breath, and leaped. This time she made it onto Brunaidh's back with a little grace, landing squarely on the blanket. Fergal handed her the stick with a shy smile. She glanced up to catch Murchad watching her, approval in his eyes. Warmth rose in Ragnhild's face.

She rode proudly down the narrow road beside her husband. The Irish warriors crowded close around her as before, giving her no opportunity to bolt as they descended the hillside.

At the base of the hill, they set off to the west on a wood-planked causeway across the marshland. It was just wide enough to accommodate two horsemen side by side. Murchad rode in the forefront, Niall at his side. Behind him, Diarmait accompanied Ragnhild. The remaining household guard was split, half of them riding behind the lead party, with a strong force bringing up the rear. Between the troops came the entourage, the baggage horses led by men and women on foot. They set the pace for the entire group.

The causeway ended on firmer ground and they followed a dirt track. When the track ended, Murchad took them deep into the hinterlands, following what seemed like deer trails that meandered through the bogs, yet he seemed to know exactly where he was going. He was heading generally northwest. Ragnhild stifled the urge to break out ahead of Murchad and run Brunaidh into the unknown.

In midafternoon, they entered a dense forest. Gloom weighed in Ragnhild's chest as she lost sight of the landscape once and for all. After following a game trail for two hours, flashes of water glinted through the brush, and they emerged on the shores of a broad lake. Far out in the middle lay an islet, bristling with trees.

Murchad and the party reined their horses, and the bannerman waved his flag. Panic rose in Ragnhild as she realized that this island was their destination.

There's no escape from this place.

She was scanning the water for a boat to come and ferry them across when Murchad nudged his horse to step out into the lake. Brunaidh followed. Ragnhild fumbled with the single rein in panic, trying to pull the pony up. She eyed the expanse of water between them and the island. Surely it was too far and too deep for the horses to swim. Ragnhild was drawing breath to shout a protest when Brunaidh's hoof grounded on something solid. Looking closely, Ragnhild detected tiny ripples on the smooth lake as the water lapped on something just below the surface. She sat in stunned silence as Brunaidh followed Murchad's horse into the lake. The pony obviously knew her way, stepping now to the left and then to the right as she followed an invisible, zigzag course. Her hooves created ripples in the still water.

A submerged stone causeway leading to a hidden fortress. She caught her breath at the cleverness of it.

As they drew near, through the leaves Ragnhild could see that live trees masked a palisade of tree trunks. They were nearly upon the wooden gate before she spied it among the foliage. It was crowned by a tower, hidden in the treetops. The gate swung open silently, revealing a phalanx of men who bowed as Murchad rode into the yard.

Within the palisade stood a thatched roundhouse, smaller than the one at Aileach. It was surrounded by several smaller buildings, some of which appeared to be living quarters, while others must be storage. The ubiquitous chickens and geese strutted about the yard, searching the ground for food.

A crowd of folk surged forward to greet them. Murchad and his men dismounted, giving their horses over to stable hands. Fergal came forward to take hold of Brunaidh's bridle, and Ragnhild slid off the pony's back. She watched her only two friends depart back across the causeway, wishing she could follow.

Murchad broke the spell. "We're home, *a chroi*. Fiona will help you settle in. I will see you this evening." He strode off with his men.

Fiona was at her elbow. She took Ragnhild firmly by the arm and conducted her across the packed-earth yard. The other Irish-women scurried along behind. They entered a smallish round-house that turned out to be the women's quarters, with the ubiquitous central hearth and alcove beds. The women, obviously at home, went to their beds and took up their spinning, chattering in Irish. Fiona showed Ragnhild to an alcove and indicated that it would be her own.

Though daylight shone through the door, reflected on the whitewashed walls, the little bower seemed too close, the women's chatter annoying. Ragnhild made for the door, ignoring Fiona's protesting noises. She pushed the door open and stepped outside into a light drizzle. Her gaze fell on the wooden tower and the ladder that leaned up against it. She hurried across the yard and scrambled up the rungs to the guard platform. The light rain freshened the air, and the incessant noise of the settlement faded. Ragnhild nodded at the astonished sentry, then turned her back on him and gazed over the placid lake and the forest beyond that stretched to the horizon. Hidden among the trees, the tower was not visible from the shore, but judicious pruning gave the sentry a broad view of the countryside. It brought home her predicament all the more clearly. *I am a prisoner in a hidden fortress in the middle of a lake, deep in the countryside, far from the river that brought me here.*

Is my crew safe? Did they escape Harald? Visions of carnage flashed in her mind. She jerked herself up short. *Wondering is a fool's occupation. Even if they've escaped, they'll never find me here. The best I can hope for is that they survive and make it home to Åsa.*

She stared down at the lake. A light breeze dappled the water, causing a faint disturbance on the surface that betrayed the causeway's zigzag path. *If I got past the gate guards, I could follow it, but the lookout would spot me long before I reached shore. It's a well-thought-out fortification.*

A few of the strange, round boats were rafted alongside a dock on the western side of the island. She eyed the tiny vessels. *Currachs.* The Irish word popped into her mind unbidden and she smiled. The fragile craft were constructed of oiled hides stretched over a framework of willow branches. Five of the seven boats looked as if they could barely support a single adult. Round as a pebble, they lacked keel or stem, and it was hard to see how they could be maneuvered with the single, broad-bladed paddle. Yet they skittered across the lake like water bugs. Two others were more substantial, dugouts hollowed from a tree trunk, able to hold perhaps four or five armed men. But they were awkward things.

The Irish ride their horses wrong, they talk wrong, their clothes are wrong, and their boats are wrong!

But, if I stole one of those boats, on a dark night...I might just make it without being seen. Hope surged for an instant, only to crash when she realized that even if she escaped, she'd never find her way to Raider Bride.

I can't speak the language, and even if I could, what Irishman would help me find a shipload of Norse raiders?

Fiona's voice sounded sharply. The Irishwoman stood at the foot of the ladder with the other three, and Ragnhild realized the sky had darkened. She had moped the afternoon away. She climbed down, following her keepers to the bower.

Fiona sat Ragnhild down on a stool and undid her snarled braid. The Irishwoman worked the comb through the knotted hair, speaking to her softly. Ragnhild's tension flowed out with the tangles. Her shoulders relaxed. She allowed the women to fuss over her, washing her face and hands with a soft cloth and replacing her encrusted tunic and breeks with a clean blue linen gown embroidered with the spirals these Irish seemed so fond of. Ragnhild refused to crack a smile, but she had to admit it was nice to be clean. Her head felt much better, released from the tight braid, and the linen gown was soothing against her skin.

Fiona brought out a green shawl of fluffy wool, draped it over Ragnhild's shoulders, and fastened it with a silver pin. With a proprietary air, the Irishwoman conducted Ragnhild out of the bower and to the main hall. Within, it was the image of the hall at Aileach in miniature, high-roofed with gold and silver ornaments glinting in the gloom. Murchad sat on the high seat, deep in conversation with Niall. His black hair gleamed and the firelight glinted on the golden torc at his throat, picking out his strong jaw and straight nose. He looked up and smiled when he saw her, eyes glittering.

"Welcome, my queen," he said, rising and stepping down off the platform to meet her. He conducted her to the seat beside his. He lifted his silver goblet to her and spoke in Irish. The others raised their glasses and their voices in response.

Servants set a feast before them, but Ragnhild's throat was tight with the knowledge that here she was truly a prisoner. A dark lump of despair had settled in the pit of her stomach.

"You must not mope, *a chroi*," said Murchad, watching her

stare down at her food. "Perhaps you need a little sport. Tomorrow, I will take you hunting."

Ragnhild cheered up at the thought of leaving the island, even under guard. The lump in her throat eased and she took a sip of ale. It slid down easily. Next she tried a bite of meat. The lamb was tender and savory. Her stomach growled in appreciation, and she demolished the rest of the meal.

When the food was gone and the last of the ale poured, she waited in fear that Murchad would expect her to accompany him to his bedchamber, but he merely toasted her and said, "Good night, wife." Then he turned back to his men.

Fiona approached. Ragnhild rose with relief and followed her and the other women to their quarters. She undressed and got into her alcove bed. The feather mattress embraced her as she tucked the soft wool coverlet around her. The Irishwomen's chatter soothed her. If she didn't listen closely, she could imagine they were her shield-maidens, getting ready for bed, murmuring in Norse.

She closed her eyes and thought of Tromøy.

IN THE MORNING she rose and hastily ate the porridge that Fiona brought her. She pulled on her tunic and breeks and hurried out to the yard, where Fergal waited with the ponies. Brunaidh nickered in greeting.

Murchad emerged from a hut with a hawk perched on his shoulder. Behind him came a man carrying another hawk.

"Good morning, *a chroí*," said Murchad. He wore a light green woolen tunic and breeks, soft deerskin boots, and a brown cloak thrown back from his shoulders, pinned with a silver brooch. He presented Ragnhild with a hunting knife. It was small, but had a sturdy handle of deer-horn and when she drew the blade from its sheath, it gleamed bright and sharp. As she slid the sheath onto her belt, her confidence surged. It was good to be armed with more than an eating knife.

She leaped onto Brunaidh's back as if she'd been doing it all her life. She donned the leather glove the falconer handed her and nudged it under the hooded hawk's feet. The bird stepped onto her glove with a tinkle of bells.

She followed Murchad out of the gate, accompanied by his hunting dog and three men-at-arms. The ponies stepped delicately in ankle-deep water, confidently following the invisible, zigzagging causeway.

Ragnhild felt light with relief to be off the island, despite the fact that she was surrounded by guards. Brunaidh's gait was buoyant, and the pony seemed to know what Ragnhild wanted from her as soon as the thought was formed.

It feels good to be understood, even by a horse.

The dog flushed some wood ducks, and Ragnhild set her hawk after them. Watching the bird soar over the lake, Ragnhild yearned to follow.

Her hawk sighted on a duck and put on a burst of power, winging through the trees with searing speed. Ragnhild's heart soared after it and she urged Brunaidh forward. With hardly a gesture from her rider, the little pony broke into a run.

The hawk struck its prey in a flurry of feathers.

Keep going. Ride!

The pony raced across the fields. The wind in Ragnhild's face drew tears from her eyes, her heart pumping to the rhythm of Brunaidh's hooves. A copse of oak trees loomed ahead. *Good cover. You can make it.*

"Ragnhild!" Murchad cried in the distance.

She didn't look back, urging Brunaidh faster. The pony was lathered with sweat but seemed to be drawn by the same spell as her rider. They gained the trees and crashed through the underbrush, branches snatching at Ragnhild's braid and slapping her cheeks.

Hoofbeats sounded behind. She dug her heels into Brunaidh's flanks. The pony stumbled and Ragnhild's heart flew into her throat, but Brunaidh recovered. The hoofbeats grew louder. Murchad rode up alongside, reaching out to grab Brunaidh's rein.

"Stop!" Murchad reined the ponies up short. "Are you trying to lame your horse?"

He slowed them to a walk to let the horses cool down. Brunaidh's eyes were ringed with white and sweat coated her heaving sides, but thank the gods, she didn't limp.

Ragnhild bowed her head to hide the tears that cascaded down her cheeks, refusing to sob.

"There, girl, calm yourself," said Murchad. She wasn't sure if he was talking to her or the horse, but his voice soothed them both. She took a few breaths and snorted like Brunaidh.

Murchad said nothing, only led them at an easy walk back to the meadow where the hawk had brought her prey to the ground and still fed on the kill.

Murchad laid his hand on Ragnhild's arm and she yanked it away instinctively, pulse hammering. "Are you all right?" he asked.

She nodded without meeting his eyes, and held out her gloved hand to accept the tender pigeon breast he drew from his pouch. She whistled and the hawk's head jerked up from the wood duck. Riveted on the pigeon breast, the bird lofted to the glove. While the hawk fed on the pigeon breast, Ragnhild secured the jesses.

As they started back, Ragnhild was still too upset to speak. Murchad seemed to know it, for though he kept his pony close enough that his knee brushed hers, he said nothing. They rode in silence, the storm in her heart gradually subsiding.

By the time they reached the causeway, Ragnhild had calmed enough to pay close attention to the location of the submerged stepping stones, memorizing how the tower bore on each one, where each turn occurred. At least she was doing something, no matter how futile.

Fergal waited in the yard with the falconer. Ragnhild gave her hawk over, but when Fergal reached for Brunaidh's rein, she shook her head, sliding off the pony's back and leading her to the water trough.

Murchad followed silently. She ignored him. While Brunaidh drank, Murchad handed Ragnhild a curry comb. She took it and gently drew it through the pony's tangled mane. Brunaidh nickered, abandoning the water trough to nuzzle her shoulder.

Murchad brought two buckets of oats and Ragnhild took one. She held it while the pony ate, wishing she could spend the night in the stable instead of the tense atmosphere of the roundhouse. But when the horses were finished, the boys took hold of their reins and led them toward the causeway. Ragnhild watched them go with longing.

Murchad laid a gentle hand on her elbow. She flinched and he drew a breath, his eyes narrowing. "You understand we are in the midst of rough country, miles from the sea or any river?"

Ragnhild nodded.

"If you run away, you could be lost in a trackless wilderness, and I might never find you."

She nodded again.

"You are my queen. I need to trust you." He fixed her with his gaze. "If I give orders for Fergal to take you ashore whenever you please, will you promise not to run away?"

Ragnhild could hardly believe what he was saying. She nodded her head.

"Then it shall be so. I don't want you to feel as if you are a prisoner here."

Yet that is what I am.

CHAPTER 13

Time passed for Behrt in a haze of pain as he lay on the heather pallet. Brother Brian fed him milk from the doe, Ethne, and oat porridge. Behrt slept much of the time, and he was sure that some of Brother Brian's herbal-scented brews eased his pain and let him sleep. During his waking time, he watched the small animals scurry in and out of the woven-branched shelter—squirrels, mice, birds. There was nothing to keep them out, and Brian encouraged them by always leaving a little pile of grain or seeds on the dirt floor for them.

"They need to eat, just like us," Brian explained as Behrt watched him pour milk in a hollowed-out depression in a stone —what Behrt's mother used to call an álf-cup.

The days went by and Behrt regained strength. Brian gradually stopped feeding him the herbal brews, but instead brought him spring water in the chipped earthen pot. Behrt's mind grew clearer, and he began to spend more time awake. He wondered what had become of Ragnhild. Had the attack on the monastery been successful in luring out the Irish king? Was *Raider Bride* on her way home already, laden with treasure? He prayed the monks had been spared.

Either way, he would never see Ragnhild again, or his ship-mates. He had no way to return to the North. He was stuck here, in the land that had rejected him.

His host was obviously too polite to ask him for personal information, but in his gentle way, Brother Brian made his guest feel as though he could talk to him. In his despair, Behrt found himself telling the hermit his story.

"I was born in Lochlainn," he said. "Near the Sogn fjord, the youngest of seven brothers. My big brothers were so strong and mighty, to me they seemed invincible as the gods. I was only nine years old when they took me to sea in their longship, on a raid to Ireland.

"My brothers were bold, but perhaps not so clever. The Irish slaughtered them all, everyone but me. Perhaps the Irish were too softhearted to kill a nine-year-old boy in cold blood. Instead, they put me in chains and dragged me to the slave market. I couldn't speak a word of Irish. When they put me up on the slave block, I was so afraid, I soiled my breeches."

"You were only a lad," said Brother Brian soothingly. "You were right to be afraid. Terrible things are done to slaves."

"But the Lord smiled on me," said Behrt. "I was purchased by a kind master, an Irish lord named Cullen, a learned man and a fair one."

Brother Brian said nothing, only smiled encouragingly, and Behrt continued his tale. "As I got bigger, my master trained me in the ways of a warrior and a Christian. I proudly served in his household guard, but Lord Cullen passed away when I was twenty.

"When my master died, he set me free in his will. But a free man means a man with no home, no people. The Irish rejected me utterly because I was a hated Norseman," he said bitterly. "So I took ship back to the country of my birth. And there I was scorned for being a Christian. I'm a man who belongs nowhere.

All I wish for is a place where I am accepted, where I can live in peace."

Brother Brian shook his head sadly. "I understand just what you are saying, my friend. I sought the very same kind of solace when I came here. The little forest creatures are my kin now. I found my place. I am sure in time you will too."

Behrt gazed at his benefactor. In many ways, he felt he'd found a kindred spirit.

Now that the pain was less, the days passed more pleasantly. Though Brother Brian was not talkative, still he was good company in his quiet way. The hermit was always busy, weeding his patch of barley, feeding the mice and birds, seeking eggs, milking Ethne.

But as Behrt began to heal, he also began to worry. He knew he couldn't impose on Brother Brian for much longer. The hermit was generous, but Behrt could see what a struggle it was for him to keep his guest fed. Brother Brian ate no meat. Ethne couldn't give much milk, rich as it was, and Brian's sack of barley was getting low. It would have to last until the next harvest, a month or more from now.

Behrt would have to find his way very soon, now that he could walk—though stagger was a more fitting term for the way he moved with the tree branch he'd carved into a walking stick.

"I thank you for your care, good friend," he said to Brother Brian. "I will be taking my leave as soon as I am able."

"And where is it you will go?" said Brian.

Where would he go? He had no weapons, no armor, no money. Could he find *Raider Bride*? He yearned to find Ragnhild and his shipmates, or at least to know their fate. By now they must have given him up for dead, and no doubt were on their way home.

At least he could speak the language. He could ask Brother Brian for directions—to where? He had lived on the west coast, far from here, where Cullen had been lord. And the folk there had made it clear they wanted nothing to do with him. The only place he knew of here was the monastery of Daire Calgach—if it was still standing. Would he be welcome there?

"There's no hurry for you to leave," said Brian soothingly. "You're good company. You're welcome here as long as you wish to stay."

"You can't keep feeding me. Your grain is getting low."

"I always have enough to feed a guest," Brian said, gesturing toward the sack of barley. It was half-full—the same as yesterday. In fact, when Behrt thought about it, it seemed that the sack had been half-full since he'd arrived. He shook his head. That wasn't possible. But his head had been addled those first few days.

Regardless of the hermit's generosity, Behrt knew he couldn't stay indefinitely. But the fear of wandering the land, alone and friendless, haunted him.

He didn't want to burden his host, so though his worries kept him awake at night, he remained silent. But Brother Brian seemed to know his fears.

"My friend," he said. "You may think your destiny is one thing when it may be something quite different. Don't worry, you'll find where you belong—sooner than you know."

EINAR WINCED as the door to the byre opened and daylight seared his eyes. The rest of the crew, those who could still move, scuttled into the shadows. Someone, no more than a silhouette in the glare, shoved a bucket of tepid, stale water in through the door, followed by another bucket with a thin, equally tepid broth that had a few lumps of unidentifiable vegetables floating in it.

Einar scrambled to the far corner to grab the slop bucket and managed to shove it into the doorway so the person couldn't shut the door without hauling away the bucket. Einar had figured that out early on when the slop bucket had overflowed in its putrid corner. With twenty-eight of them crammed inside, unable to wash and forced to share a single bucket in the dark, the byre stunk bad enough even when the bucket was emptied regularly. But after what Einar reckoned to be a week in captivity, they were used to it.

Despite the unappetizing rations, the crew hurried to slurp their ladlesful, knowing it was all they'd get for at least a day. By the daily glimpses when the door let in daylight, Einar could see they were wasting away. The wounded didn't move at all, only lay in their corners awaiting death. But Unn and her sisters, Thor bless them, refused to let them die. The women fed the wounded their ladlesful of broth and water, and did what they could to care for their wounds, but the stink in the air was flavored with the smell of rotting flesh as well as all the rest.

Before he took his turn with the ladle, Einar remembered to add another pebble to the pile he'd begun keeping the day after they'd been shut in here. He had collected seven stones, and he hoped that symbolized seven days of captivity. He tried always to add the stone when the food arrived, the only time he had enough light to locate the pile by the door. But within the dim byre, day and night blended together into an endless gray.

The crew had barely slurped their rations and returned to their spots against the wall when the door burst open again. Their captor ducked through the low frame, followed by two burly men-at-arms. Einar imagined there were more outside the byre, though in their weakened state, his crew was no threat even to three healthy, well-fed Irishmen.

"Now you tell us plans *finn gaill* raiders?" Aed demanded.

Einar shook his head, pretending not to comprehend the man's pitiful Norse.

Aed scowled and gestured one of his men forward. The warrior towered above Einar, brandishing a long knife. "You tell, or Enda hurt you."

Einar spread his hands in a gesture of helplessness, and shook his head.

Aed nodded and Enda approached one of the farm boys. Einar cringed inwardly but kept his face impassive. After the first few days, their captor discovered that torturing Einar would not elicit any information, so he ordered Enda to turn his efforts on the crew. Einar had considered fabricating a story, but the Irishmen were more likely to kill them once they thought they'd gotten the information they were after. There was no other reason to keep them alive.

But today, Enda brought out the long slave rope with nooses dangling from its coils. He looped a noose around each prisoner's neck and cinched them up tight. He and the other Irishman took hold of the rope end and hauled the prisoners to their feet, then pulled them through the door.

The captives stumbled outside, blinking in the daylight. Half a dozen Irish warriors waited in the yard, armed with spears. They poked and prodded the prisoners with their spears as Enda and his cohort dragged them toward the gate. Even the wounded were forced to hobble along.

When they stepped outside the fortress walls for the first time, Einar felt tears rise for his lost freedom. He blinked them back hastily.

The Irishmen herded them to a flax field enclosed by a waist-high wattle fence. The field was thick with weeds.

"Good farmland," murmured Unn. "Their crop is weeks ahead of ours."

One of the Irishmen demonstrated pulling weeds, then grabbed a farm boy and poked him with his spear, forcing him to the ground.

"I know how to weed," the lad snarled. He began yanking out weeds, and the others fell to their knees before their guards could provide them with similar instruction.

With dismay, Einar realized the Irish had found a use for their captives. Perhaps it would delay their inevitable deaths, but without adequate food or medical care, this hard labor would kill them off quick enough.

They toiled several days in the flax field. Einar was glad for the fine mist that tempered the summer sun. Each night they were herded back into their byre, where they dropped to the floor and lay in the dirt, too exhausted to do more than groan.

When the flax had been weeded to their captors' satisfaction, the prisoners were split up and set to other tasks—mucking out stalls, picking rocks.

Today Einar and two other lads were led to the dairy where the milkmaids handed them buckets of curds. Two guards herded them across the yard to a low opening in the defensive wall. The guard gestured for Einar to go down into the cavity. He set the bucket down and peered into the gloom, where he made out a short flight of stone stairs leading into darkness. The guard prodded him in the back with a spear. Stooping nearly double, Einar descended into the hole.

Groping the rough stones that lined the walls, Einar carefully stepped down into a small, cool room that smelled of curing meat and cheese. It was a souterrain, a cold storage room. The guard handed down a bucket of curds, which Einar took and set on the stone floor. His questing hands found shelves with crocks of butter and cream, buckets of ale and milk, and slabs of meat hanging from the ceiling.

As he lifted the bucket onto the shelf, a rat scuttled by his leg. He shuddered, but then, curious, he wondered where the rodent had gone. He shuffled his way along a stone-lined corridor that narrowed as it went deeper.

The guard called out from the entrance. Einar risked a few steps farther until suddenly his foot dangled in empty air. He grabbed the stone wall to keep from pitching into a hole. The air was colder now, with a distinct draft. It had to be coming from somewhere outside.

Einar hurried back to the entrance before the guard could come down after him and realize what he had discovered.

He'd found a way out—for all the good it would do them. There was little likelihood of an opportunity to get all twenty-eight of them to the passage. It was almost worse than not knowing—the idea of escape being so close by, with no way to get to it.

CHAPTER 14

The Crannog

Murchad kept his word and Fergal took Ragnhild across to the mainland in one of the round currachs. She stepped out onto the little boat, balancing with her bow while Fergal held her quiver of small-tipped arrows. He leaped confidently into the currach with perfect balance and sculled the little craft adeptly. She watched him closely, determined to master this skill.

They landed on the reedy shore, and she clambered out while Fergal pulled the light currach onto the beach. At her whistle, Brunaidh came galloping across the pasture, mane flying. The pony nuzzled Ragnhild as she attached the single rein to the halter and leaped onto her back. Fergal called his own mount, and flung himself astride, light as a leaf in the wind.

Ragnhild spent a blissful day rambling the countryside with Brunaidh and Fergal, relishing the sense of freedom and solitude. For those hours, she was not a prisoner. The boy made for cheerful company, chattering away in his language as they wended through a woodland filled with birdsong. Brunaidh's hooves raising the rich earthy scent of the forest floor. The gentle, ever-present mist soothed Ragnhild's skin and kept her cool, coating her hair and woolen tunic like a soft fur.

The boy was a clever game-stalker, and they each shot a brace of hares. As the daylight waned, Fergal signaled that it was time to return. She obediently trailed him to the stable, where she groomed and fed Brunaidh while Fergal tended his own horse. When she'd drawn the chores out as long as she could, Ragnhild reluctantly followed Fergal to the little boat. While he sculled back to the island, she watched the shore until the palisade cast its grim shadow over her.

Tomorrow, she promised herself.

From then on, she and Fergal took a boat to the mainland nearly every day. When Ragnhild showed interest in learning to scull, Fergal taught her, admiring her quick mastery of the craft. Ragnhild listened carefully to everything the boy said, and soon she had tucked away boating terms as well as words for woodcraft.

One morning, Murchad appeared at the dock, dressed for hunting. "I have a little free time this morning and thought I'd join you."

Ragnhild smiled at her husband. She hung back as they boarded, letting Fergal take the oar. Like the language, she wanted to keep her skill with the Irish craft a secret. Her only advantage was being underestimated.

While Fergal sculled them across the lake, she scrutinized Murchad. Though he was much older, he was strong and muscular, with no fat on his wiry frame. When the boat reached the other side, he leaped onto the shore with a nimble grace and helped Fergal drag the little craft ashore.

At the sound of his master's whistle, Murchad's horse came running with the others.

Ragnhild sprang onto Brunaidh with new grace and Murchad said, "You're learning our ways, *a chroi*."

Her face warmed at the approval in his tone. She shook off the feeling and focused on the hunt.

Murchad rode beside Ragnhild while Fergal trailed at a respectful distance. "I grew up here," he said. "This was my father's land, my inheritance. The Grianan, the Aileach Fortress, those go with the kingship. But the crannog will always be mine, and my children's." He sent her a meaningful look, which she ignored.

"I have my own land," said Ragnhild, her bitterness rising. "Left to me by my mother. Or I would if I could claim it. But that will never happen, not as long as I am prisoner here."

"You're my queen, not my prisoner."

"In my case there's little difference."

"I want you to be happy here," said Murchad.

Ragnhild snorted and urged Brunaidh ahead. They hunted the rest of the day in silence.

WHEN RAGNHILD WAS on the crannog, Fiona spent every possible moment assailing her with the language, pointing out everything from livestock to furniture to vegetables and repeating the Irish words over and over. Under the constant barrage, it was impossible for Ragnhild to avoid learning, but she kept an uncomprehending expression on her face while memorizing every word.

She soon discovered that Fiona's three companions were called Ailesh, Maire, and Orlath. The women seemed content to ignore her, chatting together as they spun their wool and flax. But they used the term *finn gaill* frequently enough, and Ragnhild knew they were talking about her. She was careful not to look up, but kept her head bent to her knife as she stroked it across the whetstone while she strove to follow their conversation.

"The *finn gaill* eats like a pig," Maire remarked.

Ragnhild fumbled the knife, snatching it back just before it hit the floor. She had understood the whole sentence.

"The way she dresses! Like a goatherd. And that tattoo on her throat!"

"Where do you think I got her clothes? She doesn't seem to know the difference." The women giggled.

"I can't imagine what the king sees in her," said Orlath.

"She's a peace-cow, nothing more," Ailesh replied. "How could such a handsome man want a woman who looks like her?"

Maire gave a knowing laugh. "I'm sure Fiona keeps him happy enough."

Ragnhild caught her breath. It hadn't occurred to her that Murchad would have other women, but she shouldn't be surprised.

Just then, Fiona swept in and the chatter stopped abruptly.

Ragnhild kept her gaze fixed on the knife clenched in her hand. How did the Irishwoman feel about serving her lover's new wife? Was Fiona aware of what a sham the marriage was? Did Murchad confide in her? A poisonous tide of humiliation rose in Ragnhild's stomach. She set her jaw. *I don't care what these Irish geese think of me. I certainly don't care if Murchad finds me attractive.*

But when Fiona took the women off to tend to the evening meal, Ragnhild went to the basin and washed her face. She unraveled her braid and combed the tangles out until the hair shone loose on her shoulders. Then she donned the blue linen gown and made her way to the hall.

The women fell silent as she entered. Murchad looked up and stared. He rose from his seat and came to meet her. "My lady," he murmured in Norse, taking her hand and conducting her to the high seat. "You look like a goddess."

Ragnhild ignored his compliment and kept a stone face, but she felt the blush creep up her neck. She took her seat haughtily and accepted the cup Fiona brought her.

She sipped at the ale, keeping her expression vacant while straining to follow the men's discussion. Niall and Diarmait had departed and now Murchad conversed with his men-at-arms. Their words were nothing Fiona had taught her, and by the end of the evening her head ached from struggling to grasp their conversation. However, she had managed to memorize a few useful terms relating to war and tactics.

When the feasting was done, Ragnhild rose to retire with her women. Murchad looked up from his conversation as she stood, giving her a smile and a quick nod. If he was dissatisfied with their chaste relationship, he didn't show it.

Fiona must keep him happy indeed.

The women were unusually quiet as they entered their quarters and settled into their alcoves. Ragnhild lay awake long into the night, wishing she were back on Tromøy. Would she ever see Åsa and her shield-maidens again? Queen or no, she would never fit in with these Irish.

The next day Ragnhild walked into the hall as Murchad was berating Fiona. "My wife must speak our language. Your queen must be able to speak to her people."

"She won't learn. She's dumb as a rock," Fiona said. "I am at my wit's end. I don't know what more to do."

Ragnhild kept her face blank as they turned to her in surprise. Fiona's expression changed from horrified to relieved when Ragnhild gave no sign of understanding. Murchad's gaze fastened on her in a way that made her fidget.

"It's nice to see the roses back in your cheeks," he said in Norse.

Ragnhild felt a surge of warmth for him, but it would not do to show it. She nodded curtly, then gathered bread and a crock of ale from the table and stalked back out into the yard.

She climbed the tower ladder, smiling a greeting to the guards. She offered them ale and bread, and sat down to share it with them as she had a few times before. Though she could not really converse, she'd gotten to know each of their names. After several afternoons with them, watching their routine, she knew when the guards changed, which men were most vigilant, and which were careless.

But as she gazed out over the lake to the vast forest and trackless bogland, her feeling of accomplishment dissolved. She was lost. There were no rivers to follow, no coastline with bays and islands. Just trees and marsh as far as she could see.

Where was Raider Bride and her crew? Had they survived? Or has my bastard brother caught them and slaughtered them? I will find a way to get to Harald and take vengeance on him and everyone who has betrayed me. Kol, for certain, along with everyone at Birsay. She pictured their hall in flames.

Did that include Signy? Her heart contracted at the thought. She was Harald's wife, but though their acquaintance had been brief, Ragnhild had felt a connection with her Christian sister-in-law.

And what of Orlyg? Had her younger brother betrayed her? The idea hit like a fist in the gut. They'd been inseparable all through childhood. If Harald had destroyed that bond, she'd cut his heart out and make him eat it.

A flicker of movement on shore caught her eye. The sentry, a man named Dara, had seen it too. The shore patrol came into view, leading a party of half a dozen horsemen. Dara called down to another man who dashed to the main hall.

A few moments later, Murchad emerged from the roundhouse, strapping on his sword, and bounded up the ladder. He squinted at the banner in the dwindling light. "It's Aed mac Neill. Send a boat for them."

So, Murchad does not trust this visitor enough to reveal the causeway to him. Ragnhild tucked this piece of information carefully away.

The newcomers were ferried over in one of the larger currachs, leaving their horses with the shore watch. As their boat reached the dock, Murchad descended the ladder to greet them. Ragnhild scrambled down after him.

Murchad opened his arms to the leader of the visiting party and greeted him in Irish, then turned to her. "May I present my queen, Ragnhild," he said, then switched to Norse as he addressed her. "This man is called Aed mac Neill, chieftain of Tullynavin." Ragnhild inclined her head, silently repeating the strange names.

"A *finn gaill!*" Aed stared at Ragnhild's tatoo with obvious revulsion. She smiled at him inanely, giving no sign that she understood.

"Yes, she is sister to King Harald of Lochlainn," said Murchad.

"So you are now kin to our enemy." Aed spat the words.

Murchad bristled. "Enemies no longer. We are allies now."

"If you can trust a *finn gaill*," scoffed Aed.

"If you prefer, you can consider her a hostage."

Ragnhild froze, her face a smiling mask. A hostage. Of course, that's all she was. What a fool she was not to have realized it before.

Did Murchad realize how little value she was to Harald? All her brother really wanted was to get her out of the way. In spite of his gallant manners, if Murchad knew the truth, how much would her life be worth?

The men kept talking without looking her way, and she strained to follow their words. She caught the name Conchobar repeatedly, as well as Niall and Diarmait. A welter of unintelligible names of men and places she knew nothing of slid past her ears. But one remark caught her attention.

"Our currachs captured a *finn gaill* ship," said Aed.

Ragnhild's heart leaped, but she kept her gaze lowered. One ship.

It could be *Raider Bride*.

"And what have you done with the heathen?" asked Murchad.

"We are holding them prisoner in the rath, trying to get information from them about the plans of the *finn gaill* raiders."

"What have they told you?"

Aed shook his head. "Nothing so far, but we have not killed any of them yet. Right now we are working them in the fields." He shrugged. "When I return, we'll start killing them, one by one. That should make them talk. And if not..." He shrugged again.

Ragnhild choked back a gasp. She clenched her hands into fists to still their trembling and stared at the ground, taking a few deep breaths to slow her pounding heart.

She had to get to her crew.

This could be her opportunity. When these visitors left, she could slip away and follow them to the place her ship and crew were being held. Then she would find a way to free them.

The chance was slim, but she had to take it.

As Murchad led the visitors to the hall, she fled to the women's quarters, where she forced herself to hold still as Fiona dressed her in the silk leine and fussed with her hair. After the Irishwoman turned her loose, Ragnhild entered the hall in a daze and took her place beside Murchad, her mind awhirl. Smiling vaguely, she concentrated on the men's talk, but no one mentioned the *finn gaill* ship again.

The visit dragged on for two more days. Each night they feasted. Ragnhild sat beside her husband, eyes trained on her ale cup as she strained to follow the men's conversation. During the day while the visitors were closeted with Murchad in the hall, she made preparations for her escape.

Murchad had not given back her sword, so she armed herself with a bow, a quiver of arrows, and the hunting knife. She filled a leather flask with water and a saddlebag with dried meat and flatbread.

Nestled in the bottom of the saddlebag was the great golden necklace Murchad had given her. Ragnhild considered looting the church, but the silver ornaments were bulky and hard to carry. The necklace was more valuable than everything on the altar, and it was rightfully hers.

It belongs to the rightful queen of Aileach, came a niggling thought.

That's who I am. And I owe Murchad nothing. It's mine.

When at last Aed announced his intention to depart in the morning, Ragnhild was ready. Just before dawn, she collected Brunaidh's tack and hid it with her provisions and weapons under a tarp in the smallest currach. As she'd hoped, the sentries were busy in the yard along with everyone else. By torchlight, men hauled the baggage out of the guest house and others filled saddlebags with provisions.

As the sun rose, Murchad and his guests emerged from the roundhouse. Ragnhild took her place beside her husband to exchange hearty farewell speeches on the dock while servants and men-at-arms bustled about, loading baggage and provisions into the big currach.

At last Aed and his men boarded. She watched Fergal get into the boat with the other stable boys to help with the guest's horses. She waved as the boatman shoved off.

"I'll be going ashore for my ride," she said to Murchad, praying he would be too preoccupied to join her. "I'll meet up with Fergal on the other side."

"Very well," he said, and turned to go back into the hall.

Ragnhild breathed a sigh of relief as she got into the currach and pushed away from the dock into the lake. She sculled to the mainland and dragged the boat into the reeds, concealing it so that Fergal would not see it. She hoped no one would think of it again until she failed to appear that evening.

Brunaidh appeared, her breath warm on Ragnhild's cheek as she nuzzled her. The pony stood patiently as Ragnhild put on her bridle and slung the blanket across her back along with her bags. Brunaidh made no objection to the added weight of supplies and bedroll.

Ragnhild stayed hidden while Fergal and the other stable lads rounded up the guest's horses and bridled them. Brunaidh kept still, seeming to sense the need for silence. Once the visitors were mounted, the stable boys, including Fergal, boarded the boat to go back to the crannog, while the visitors set out on the forest trail.

When Aed's party was out of earshot, Ragnhild mounted Brunaidh and followed, keeping downwind so the horses would not catch her scent and trailing far enough behind to elude the Irish rear guard. Fortunately it was a soft day, the air filled with a fine mist that muffled their scent, dampening the leaves on the ground so they didn't crackle. Brunaidh stepped delicately through the underbrush, barely turning a leaf.

Ragnhild looked back constantly for signs of pursuit, but the day wore on and there were none. She congratulated herself. So far, her plan seemed to be holding together.

When the Irish party stopped for the night, Ragnhild let Brunaidh graze while she made a cold camp. She knew the pony would stay close by.

Cocooned in her blanket, she watched the distant glow of their fire flicker through the trees. Snatches of laughter drifted back to her. A sense of loss nagged at the edges of her thoughts. She found herself missing the Irishwomen's chatter, even if they were insulting her, and Fiona's solicitous care, though that had taken on a new meaning.

By now, Murchad would have realized she was gone. He'd be angry, certainly. With a pang, she hoped he wouldn't take it out on Fergal. She wished she could have taken the boy with her.

Murchad would guess that she was following Aed's party. Would he come after her? Or was he in the arms of Fiona, without a thought for his missing queen? Perhaps he was relieved that she was gone.

Brunaidh approached, her footfalls soft on the forest floor. The pony nickered softly, lipping Ragnhild's ear. An earthy scent rose from the humus of dried leaves and pine needles. The long day's ride and the tension of tracking, while remaining undetected, had worn Ragnhild out. The pony's reassuring presence soothed her, and she drifted off to sleep.

She woke to birdsong. Refreshed from sleeping in the night air, she was up and ready while the Irish party was still at their breakfast. They were in no hurry as they packed up and set off.

At mid-morning, a stillness came over the forest that warned Ragnhild someone was following. She branched off and found a glade deep in the wood to tether Brunaidh, then doubled back on foot. She climbed a tree and waited, arrow nocked in her bow.

The faintest rustle in the undergrowth told her a rider approached. As the man on horseback came near, Ragnhild drew her bow and took aim.

It was Murchad.

She had been expecting him, but her heart beat hard all the same.

He was alone. He was stalking her, and that required the stealth of a lone hunter. As he passed beneath her, she held her breath.

For a moment, she wanted to reach out and touch him. Her hand quivered on the string.

When he had passed out of sight, she exhaled and lowered her bow. She scrambled out of the tree and back to Brunaidh, then set out after Murchad, following him as he tracked the Irish party, and her, or so he thought.

She felt smug to be stalking her hunter.

After a couple of hours, Murchad halted. Ragnhild looped Brunaidh's rein around a tree branch and crept close to watch him. He sat his horse heavily, his shoulders hunched.

Then he turned his mount and headed back toward home.

Ragnhild shrank into the foliage as he rode past, getting a clear view of his face. The lines seemed to sag, making him look older. As he disappeared into the forest, a gloom descended on her.

I could still go back.

She imagined bursting from cover like a game bird, running up behind him. He'd turn in surprise, his features lifting into a smile.

But she didn't move.

A dullness settled over her. She remounted Brunaidh and followed Aed's party for the rest of the day, trailing them through the forest. Her mind kept turning to Murchad.

In the late afternoon, they broke out of the forest. Hanging back in the verge of the woodland, Ragnhild sighted a fortress in the distance, crowning a low hill that overlooked a river. Like Murchad's crannog, the enclosure was circular, protected by a timber palisade mounted on an earthen embankment. A deep ditch surrounded the bank, and the gate could only be reached by a short wooden bridge. And like the crannog, the gate was surmounted by a watchtower.

Ragnhild kept to the trees, watching the Irish party as they rode up the hill and hailed the tower watch. At their approach, the fortress's gates swung open. They clattered across the bridge into the fort, and Ragnhild glimpsed a scattering of the familiar round, thatched buildings.

The gates closed behind them, and she turned her attention to the river nearby. Trees grew thickly along the bank on both sides, but the land surrounding the fort was an open plain that led down to the river. A lone sentry guarded a rickety-looking dock, with several of their flimsy craft moored to it. Ragnhild scanned the fleet, and her heart gave a lurch.

Among the currachs reared a longship's prow, the dragon's head still mounted on the stem.

Raider Bride.

Ragnhild stared at her ship, longing rising in her. *I will reclaim my ship as well as my crew*, she vowed. *And then I will take vengeance on Harald and take my inheritance.*

Then she turned away and led Brunaidh deeper into the forest. Some distance from the fort she found a spot where the trees grew right down to the riverbank. Under their cover she led the pony down to drink.

She left Brunaidh to graze in the forest while she stole closer to the fort. Beside it was another circular enclosure, and she watched the Irish lead their cattle and horses in for the night. The gates to the main fort opened for them, and Ragnhild longed to slip inside. The crew of *Raider Bride* was within those walls. Were they still alive? And if they were, how would she get in to free them? The fort was surrounded by an open plain, making it difficult for her to approach unseen, even at night. And even if she did, how would she cross the ditch and scale that palisade?

She watched until near sunset, but no opportunity presented itself. As evening fell, she returned to Brunaidh and made her cold camp beneath the trees. She fell into an uneasy sleep, waking at every rustle and twig snap.

Suddenly she jerked awake, gripping her knife.

Murchad sat at her side, gazing down at her.

"Good morning, *a chroi*," he said with a smile.

CHAPTER 15

Tullynavin

Ragnhild stared at him, speechless. He had somehow doubled back to follow her. He must have been behind her all along and she had not noticed, so certain she had fooled him.

"Did you think I would ever abandon you, *a mhuirin?*" he crooned. "Don't feel badly, love. This is my native land, after all. I've been hunting and scouting here since I was a lad. And you are new to these parts."

Ragnhild hid her humiliation with a scowl. "You could have captured me at any time. Why didn't you?"

"It's true, I could have taken you by force—but I would get no happiness from that. You are clever, *a chroi!* I know for certain I never mentioned your ship and crew in Norse. You have learned our language and kept it a secret all this while."

Ragnhild was stunned. She had misjudged this man utterly. He had pretended to be a simple, trusting, somewhat foolish man, but that was far from the truth. He'd duped her from the very beginning. To be a king, especially in this country, a man must be cunning and duplicitous, and that her husband was.

"What do you want from me?" she blurted in frustration.

"To have you come back to me," he said simply.

She wouldn't be fooled again by his sweet words. "I won't abandon my crew to your countrymen."

"No, I see that, and that is why I've let you come this far," said Murchad.

"I won't leave them."

"If you could, I would have been able to let you go." Murchad had a look in his eyes she had never seen before. Sad? No. More like wistful.

Then he shook himself like a dog and sprang to his feet, reaching a hand out to her. "Remember, I promised to let your crew go free. I think it is time for Tullynavin to receive a visit from their king and queen."

Shock coursed through her for the second time. He held all the advantages, and now he was giving her exactly what she sought. What was he up to?

Without a word she mounted Brunaidh and they rode across the plain to the fortress gates, where Murchad hailed the tower watch.

The gates creaked open. Ragnhild was still too stunned to speak. She had racked her brain futilely to find a way to get inside these walls, and now she rode into the fortress at Murchad's side, the denizens of Tullynavin bowing as they passed.

Aed stared at them, slack-jawed and pop-eyed, apparently completely undone by their appearance. Then he snapped his mouth shut and jackknifed into a low bow.

"My lord...and lady," he stuttered as he unbent his lanky frame and straightened up. "I had not expected to see you again so soon."

Murchad dismounted and Ragnhild followed his example. At

a nod from Aed, a stable hand came forward and led their horses away.

"I had a mind to question these heathen prisoners of yours," Murchad said smoothly.

"Why, of course, Lord," Aed stammered. "But please, come to the hall and refresh yourselves first."

"I am eager to see the heathens," Murchad insisted. "Then we will gladly partake of your hospitality."

"As you wish, of course," Aed said in honeyed tones belied by his sour look. He led them across the yard of hard-packed earth to a hovel that looked like a cow byre. "I warn you, they are not a pretty sight." He pushed the door open and motioned them inside.

The stench hit in a wave. Ragnhild's heart hammered as she peered into the gloom at the huddled forms who shrank from the light flooding in the door. When her eyes adjusted to the dimness, she drew a sharp breath at the sight of the filthy creatures cowering in the shadows. Could this really be the crew of *Raider Bride*?

Murchad squeezed her hand and shot her a look, reminding her to stifle her reaction. He turned to Aed, who remained outside the byre and upwind. "I will question these heathens now. I am sure you have much to do in preparation for our welcome. There is no need for you to stay." He waved their host off.

"Of course, my lord," said Aed, his face clearing as he scurried off.

"Einar!" Ragnhild hissed, ducking through the low door. "Unn!"

"Ragnhild, is it really you?" Unn's voice was little more than a quaver and the sound of it struck ice in her heart.

She strained to make out their condition in the dim byre. "Yes, it's me. Tell me how you fare."

"Lady," Einar said, coming hesitantly into the light. He was filthy from head to toe, his tunic ragged, hair matted. From what she could see, the others were in no better shape. "Your brother attacked us and we lost six. Four more are wounded, though they are still alive. But the Irish are working us to death. We've had almost nothing to eat for days, and only rank water to drink."

"Come into the light, all of you," Ragnhild said.

She examined the injured, unwinding their dirty, makeshift bandages and sniffing at the wounds. The stench of rot was faint but worrying. They were half-starved, all of them, with trembling hands and parched lips.

She turned to Murchad. "Can we get them some ale, and something to eat?"

"Yes, food and ale," he said. "They must gain their strength. They'll need to be able to travel."

She stared at him. What was he planning?

Murchad grinned at her. "Come, we must attend our host."

"I'll be back to see you as soon as I can," she said to Einar. "We'll send food and ale."

She hurried to catch up with her husband, who was already striding across the yard to the hall, where, at an order from Murchad, food and drink was dispatched to the Norse prisoners.

"What were you thinking, man?" he said to Aed. "They're half-dead with hunger. I can't get a sensible word out of them."

Aed accepted the rebuke with some grace and ushered them into the guest house. The women of the fort surrounded Ragnhild and took her off to their quarters, where they clucked over her breeks and tunic, filthy from sleeping rough. They laid out a green linen gown, then undressed her and bathed her like a child, chattering as Ragnhild pretended not to understand.

"She's tall," one exclaimed.

"And muscular as a man. And those tattoos!"

"But she appears to be female under all that dirt." They broke out into giggles as Ragnhild kept her face blank.

"Dumb as a post, isn't she?"

"Yes. Lord knows what King Murchad sees in a giantess like her."

"He only married her for the treaty with the other heathens."

"That explains a lot. Poor Murchad! Can you imagine what it must be like to bed her?"

They broke into laughter once again. Ragnhild resisted the urge to scowl, but she could do nothing about the flush that crept up her throat and spread to her face.

They wrapped her in a linen sheet and sat her on a low stool. One of the Irishwomen unbraided the ratty plait. As she picked up the antler comb, the door opened and Murchad strode in. The women froze, eyes downcast. He stepped forward and held out his hand for the comb. "Allow me."

The Irishwoman relinquished the comb, and the entire flock backed toward the door, bowing their way out of the room.

Murchad smiled down at her. "May I?"

Ragnhild nodded. She sat stiffly while Murchad plied the comb through her chaotic hair. Starting at the bottom, he patiently untangled snarls, working his way up to her scalp. At the gentle tugging, Ragnhild's eyes closed and her tension drained away.

"You have such beautiful hair," said Murchad. "Soft and shining."

Ragnhild stiffened and jerked the comb out of his hand. She rose and stalked to a corner where she yanked the teeth through her hair.

"I'm sorry, I didn't mean to offend you," he said.

Ragnhild glared at him. She turned her back and continued to ply the comb. When her hair was tangle-free, she pulled the linen gown on, then peered over her shoulder and caught her breath. Murchad, his back to her, had stripped to the waist. Ragnhild stared as he ran the washcloth over his lean, well-muscled torso. The battle scars tracked across the white skin of his back. She wondered what it would be like to run her hands over those scars.

As if he felt her scrutiny, Murchad turned toward her and she hastily averted her gaze.

"You look lovely, wife."

Ragnhild scowled at the gown, delicately embroidered at the hem and sleeves. She stared as Murchad pulled on a splendid linen robe trimmed with tablet-woven bands. He shook back his black hair and smiled at her, offering his arm. "Shall we?"

She laid her hand on his forearm and let him lead her into the hall.

The folk of Tullynavin were already assembled on their benches. They raised a cheer as their king and queen entered and mounted the platform. Murchad accepted a goblet from a servant and raised it.

A hasty meal had been laid out. Murchad sat in an ornately carved chair which Ragnhild felt sure was usually Aed's place. Murchad shot her an approving look as she took her place beside him.

Hurried as it was, the hot meal of meat and cabbage was a luxury after the scant rations on the trail, and Ragnhild partook with good appetite, paying little attention to the conversation until she was finished. After the meal was cleared, while they relaxed with their mead, Murchad leaned over to his host. "I will take the heathens back with me for questioning."

'But, Lord King…" Aed said with ill-disguised dismay.

"My Norse queen can communicate with them as none of us can," Murchad went on, oblivious, "and of course, as your king, these captives are mine to do with as I wish." Murchad gave Aed a pointed grin which Ragnhild pretended to ignore, though it kindled a flame of hope in her.

The stress slid off Ragnhild's shoulders as she drank and laughed. Soon they'd depart with her crew. They should be able to get away from Murchad easily, sail away in *Raider Bride* and wreak havoc on Harald.

The feast dragged on. The skáld's—or rather, the bard's—entertainment caused Ragnhild's eyes to glaze over. She was glad to pretend she couldn't follow his foolish tales of ancient Irish heroes—men who seemed to have nothing better to do than steal each other's cattle.

At last the evening came to a close and Aed conducted Ragnhild and Murchad to their quarters, a partitioned chamber dominated by a huge feather bed. When they were alone, Murchad said, "After your crew has recovered enough to travel, they will accompany us back to the crannog."

"I thank you for that, my lord," she said.

He smiled, setting his green eyes afire. "I gave you my word, a *chroi.* I will always keep my word to you."

Her heart beat harder at his words. He was one of the few men in her life who'd kept his word to her. It was a shame she'd have to leave him so soon. If only their circumstances had been different.

She wanted to touch him. This may well be the last night she'd have with him. She'd never let a man touch her. He was her husband, and she wanted him to be the first.

His eyes widened as she approached him. He seemed to hold his breath when she laid a hand on his arm. Then his arms went around her and he pulled her to him, his mouth finding hers. His kiss was soft and a wave of pleasure surged through her.

He drew back, his breath coming as hard as her own, and gazed into her eyes. "Are you sure?" he murmured.

"Yes," she said, knowing well what was coming. There was little privacy in the longhouse she'd grown up in, and she'd seen men and women together many times, though no man had ever dared approach her.

Murchad kissed her tattoo. "You're so strong, a *chroi,*" he murmured. "So brave. I've never known a woman like you." His warm breath on her neck evoked a shiver that ran down her spine. She let him back her toward the bed. He lifted her gown and her arms went up. She pressed the length of her body against him. He pulled her leine over her head and let it drop to the floor. He ran his hands down her sides, covering her face and neck with kisses, and she let the pleasure lap through her like waves on a beach.

His hands were gentle, sensitive to her smallest reaction. He knew when to hold her softly and when his grip should be firm. His every touch was exactly what she desired, and left her wanting more.

A tiny warning sounded in her head, but it was easy to ignore as she kissed him and unbuckled his belt.

IN THE MORNING, the women woke Ragnhild. Murchad was already gone, his place beside her empty and cold.

As she dressed, Ragnhild tried to ask for clean bandages and water, but she didn't know the Irish words and the women seemed not to understand her, whether real or pretended. In frustration, she stormed out to find Murchad.

He was in the yard, speaking with Aed. Their backs were to her and they hadn't seen her yet. The sight of her husband kindled a flame within her.

But that flame was extinguished by his next words to Aed. "You may provide me with a suitable escort, say thirty men, to keep the heathens under control."

Ragnhild's heart plummeted. The clever bastard had tricked her again. She was still his prisoner. What a fool she was.

Now we are all your prisoners. She forced herself to smile and take heart. Perhaps there was another way. If she watched and waited, surely an opportunity would present itself. She had found her crew against all the odds. It was a long journey through the Irish countryside to the crannog, ripe with possibilities. Fed and rested, the Norse might be able to overcome their escort and escape. And she knew the land much better now.

She approached the two men as if she'd just arrived and hadn't heard their conversation. "Good morning, husband," she said in Norse. "I can't seem to make the women understand me. I need clean bandages, clean water for washing, and herbs and salves."

Murchad turned to Aed and relayed her request, but then he turned back to her. "I've asked for bandages and washing water, but I'm not sure what else you are asking for."

Ragnhild grabbed up a weed growing in the courtyard and shook it at him. Murchad looked even more puzzled. "Healing herbs, salves!" Ragnhild had no idea what the Irish words were.

Murchad only stared at her uncomprehendingly, his Norse obviously beyond its limits. She stomped her foot and swore an oath that made Murchad's eyebrows shoot up and the servants scatter. Ragnhild stormed off to visit her crew.

They looked a bit better than the day before, and a few were sitting up and speaking. The food and ale seemed to have made a difference already.

"I'm worried," said Unn. "Some of the wounds smell like they're beginning to fester."

Ragnhild nodded. "I noticed that yesterday. I've asked for clean bandages and washing water. I tried to get some herbal salves, but I couldn't make them understand."

Ragnhild's message must have gotten across to someone, for half an hour later an Irishwoman appeared at the hovel's door carrying a basket covered with a linen cloth. She entered timidly, but Unn's friendly smile set her at ease. The Norse girl lifted the linen cover and peered into the basket, sniffing herbs and pots of salve. She nodded enthusiastically, swept the Irishwoman up in a hug and dragged her over to the wounded. Within minutes the two were communicating through sign language and trading the names of herbs and remedies.

A slave arrived with a bucket of washing water and lengths of clean linen for bandages. Unn and the Irishwoman began to tend wounds while Ragnhild conferred with Einar, Thorgeir, and Svein in low tones. "Murchad is taking us all back to his fortress soon. We will travel under an armed guard. Everyone must be ready, and watch for our opportunity to escape on the way."

"It would be much better if we could get away in *Raider Bride*," said Einar. "Trying to flee overland on foot is a recipe for failure."

Ragnhild ground her teeth in frustration. "You're right, of course. But how can we escape from this stronghold? The gate and walls are well-guarded and we're surrounded by a deep ditch."

Einar spoke up. "There's an underground storeroom in the wall. I was down there one day to bring up food and a rat ran by me. It disappeared into the depths. I followed the rat to the far end and I swear I felt a draft. I am positive there's a tunnel that leads outside the fort."

"I'll search for it," said Ragnhild. Feeling encouraged, she helped clean and bandage wounds and lift spirits with a little gentle teasing.

"Much better," said Unn, surveying the wounded with satisfaction. "I think we may save them all."

One of the women came to fetch Ragnhild to make ready for the evening's feast. As she crossed the yard, Ragnhild felt the pull of *Raider Bride*. She climbed to the platform and gazed over the palisade at the dragon's head rising among the currachs. She yearned to step aboard her ship again. It was all she could do not to run down to the dock and cast off.

Soon, she thought. *I'll find a way.*

Aed entertained his king and queen with fair grace, no doubt relieved that there were only two of them to feed instead of a king's customary retinue. He'd slaughtered a bullock and fed them well. The Irish flavored their ale with different herbs than the juniper berries Ragnhild was accustomed to, but she found it drinkable. When the bard declaimed the silly antics of their Irish heroes, she refrained from rolling her eyes, instead allowing them to glaze over.

When Murchad came to her that night, she steeled herself to pretend that nothing had changed.

"What's wrong?" he said.

"Nothing," she answered, and drew him down to her, distracting him with a kiss. He pulled her close and soon her body responded to his touch, despite her feelings of betrayal.

In the morning she woke to find Murchad gone again. Relieved that she didn't have to face him, Ragnhild donned her woolen breeks and tunic and visited her crew. Their spirits were much better now, with bellies full and wounds cleaned and tended. When she had spoken to each one of them, she left to find the tunnel Einar had told her of.

She circumnavigated the palisade, looking for the opening in the foundation, while not appearing to be searching at all. Every time someone came by, she feigned admiration for the squat, thatched roundhouses or inspected a flock of ducks. Though the inhabitants gave her plenty of stares, they did not seem suspicious.

In the early afternoon, her search finally paid off. She noticed a servant emerging from a rock-lined opening low down on the wall.

Glancing around to be sure no one was watching, she got to her knees and peered into the entrance. After a moment her eyes adjusted to the gloom. Below her, stairs descended into darkness. She lowered herself into the cold storage room and edged her way to the far end.

She shuffled along a stone-lined corridor that narrowed, just as Einar had described, and then her sliding foot met nothing but air. Her heart thudded and she grabbed the wall to keep herself from falling. Getting to her knees, she felt around the drop-off, staring down into the hole. Inside, it was dark as a well, going straight down into blackness.

Ragnhild sat and lowered her feet into the hole. They dangled in the air, finding no bottom to the shaft. A shiver ran through her. It was like the entrance to Hel.

She shook off the foolish thought and felt around the floor for a pebble. She let it drop. The sound it made when it hit bottom told her the hole was not too deep.

She took a breath and eased herself into the dark.

Her feet hit bottom a couple of feet down. Now she was in complete darkness, but a sweep of her foot traced an opening low down. Ragnhild squatted and scuttled into the passage on all fours.

Shrugging off a shudder, she set out crawling. The low tunnel was lined with dank, rough stones that bruised her knees. The air smelled of must, and she was glad it was too dark to see what else was down there.

Suddenly her hands floundered into open air below her.

Another hole.

She dropped another stone and heard a reassuring plop. This passage was too narrow to allow her to squirm around and get her feet in front of her. She would have to go in head first. Stretching her arms out in front of her, she swallowed hard and plunged into the darkness. Her hands slammed into the rock floor, sending a jolt of pain through her elbows and shoulders as she slithered into another low tunnel.

In a short distance the bottom dropped away again. This time she lowered herself into the hole more gently, slowing her fall by bracing her legs along the passage wall. Still the rock surface rasped across her hands.

By now she reckoned she must be beneath the ditch that surrounded the fortress. The tunnel straightened out for a long way, and she realized it was gradually climbing. The passage grew steeper. She crawled on, her hands and knees chafed raw.

And then she ran head first into a wall.

Blood trickled down her face and her forehead pounded. It was a dead end. She would have to go back, but there was no room to turn around. Icy fingers of panic gripped her heart.

A cool draft kissed her left cheek, and she realized that the passage made a sharp turn here. She crawled to her left, then hit a wall again. This time the passage branched off to her right. Making her way into it, she was rewarded by a glimmer of daylight. She scurried toward the light like a rat in a tunnel. The passage ascended once again.

Branches stabbed her face. She backed up, spitting, then realized she'd run into a shrub. Ragnhild shoved her way around it, ignoring the scratches and scrapes as she clambered out of the exit hole and scrambled to her feet.

Stretching her sore limbs in relief, she looked around. It appeared that she had come out somewhere in the woods. Creeping through the trees to the forest edge, she peered out into the clearing and saw the palisade. The gate tower rose on the opposite side of the wall. She was looking at the backside of the fort. That meant that her position was hidden from the watch's sight. From here, she might be able to lead her crew down to the ship under cover of darkness.

Eager to share her news, she crept back into the passage. Now that she knew its secrets, her fear was gone. Ignoring the raw sting of her abraded knees and hands, she made her way back through the tunnel quickly. When she scrambled back into the cold storage room, she peered out of the opening to make sure only ducks and geese noted her passage. Then she climbed out and hurried to the cow byre.

"I've found the way out of the fort," she announced breathlessly. She had everyone's attention. "But it gets narrow. We'll have to crawl through a stone-lined passageway that twists and turns." She looked at Unn. "Will they be able to make it?"

Unn assessed the wounded. "Bjarni took a bad blow to the head. He battles terrible headaches that come and go, and they can last for hours, but even so he should be able to keep up." She nodded at the two with lacerated legs. "These two can also manage, though crawling on the rough stones will cause them considerable pain. My main concern is with Alm. He still can't put any weight on his dislocated shoulder."

Ragnhild looked Alm in the eye. "It's a long way on hands and knees. Are you up to it?"

He nodded. "I may be a little slower, but I can move along like a three-legged dog." He proceeded to demonstrate. He did manage to crawl across the floor, but he was so slow and clumsy that Ragnhild was filled with doubt.

Einar must have read her expression. "We'll make it," he said. "I'll drag the lad if nothing else."

Ragnhild was full of misgivings, but she could see no options.

That evening Murchad informed Aed that they would depart in the morning.

They were out of time.

CHAPTER 16

A cold rain hit Behrt in the face. He reached for the heather to cover himself and found none.

His eyes flew open, blinking in the cold light. He was lying on bare ground, completely exposed to the weather.

Behrt sat up, amazed to find himself alone on a hilltop. Where was the forest? Where was Brother Brian? How had he gotten here? He couldn't remember leaving the forest.

Tales of folk kidnapped by the faeries rose in his mind—when the Sidhe were done with you, they left you abandoned in the open, to find years had passed.

He shook off the thought and scrambled to his feet. A wave of dizziness swept through him, roiling his stomach. He fought down nausea while trying to focus on the surrounding country-side. A river snaked along to the east—it must be the Feabhail, he thought. Swampland stretched in all other directions. At the base of the hill he stood on, a stone causeway crossed the bog to another hill to the east, another island in the bog, crowned with a ringed enclosure. Within the walls, robed figures moved among thatched buildings. A High Cross carved in stone towered in their midst.

The monastery of Daire Calgach.

It was raining much harder now, and the ground had turned to mud. His walking stick was gone, but he tried a few steps and found he didn't need it. He set out down the hill, slogging through the mud toward the monastery. They would give him shelter. All monasteries maintained guest houses for weary travelers.

The brother at the gate welcomed him. Without his boots or weapons, nothing marked him as a Norse warrior. Behrt's accent was recognizable as from the west coast of Ireland. His woolen tunic and bare feet were no different from the clothing many Irish men wore.

"I am Brother Padraig," said the monk.

"My name is Becc mac Cullen." Behrt gave the Irish name his master had given him, hoping it would suffice. "I am a traveler seeking a place to sleep for the night."

The monk, obviously used to travelers from all over, did not seem concerned with Behrt's name. "Yes, of course, follow me." Brother Padraig led him across the yard to a large thatched roundhouse.

Inside, a fire crackled on the central hearth, scenting the air cleanly. Behrt moved as close to the fire as he dared, until steam rose off his tunic with a whiff of sodden wool.

"Get out of those wet clothes before you catch your death," said Brother Padraig. "I will find you something to wear." He bustled out of the room.

The guest house was bare but comfortable, with half a dozen straw-stuffed sleeping pallets against the whitewashed walls. A simple wooden table and three stools stood near the hearth. Behrt huddled on one of the stools, shivering.

Brother Padraig brought in a bowl of warm water and a linen towel and set them on the table. Then he laid out a monk's habit on one of the pallets. "You can wear this until your clothes dry. I will leave you to refresh yourself, and bring you something to eat." The monk bowed and left him.

Behrt peeled off his sodden tunic and breeks, and took his time washing his hands and face, luxuriating in the warm water. He picked up the monk's habit and slipped the robe over his head. The coarse wool slid down his body, suffusing him with warmth.

Brother Padraig returned with a welcome cup of ale and a wooden plate of bread and cheese. Behrt tried not to fall on the food like a ravenous wolf, but his stomach commanded otherwise.

The monk waited politely until he'd finished. "The abbot wishes to see you," he said. Behrt followed Brother Padraig back out into the rain. They followed a stone path across a courtyard of hard-packed earth. The entire yard had a slight camber that drained the rainwater away from the center to a shallow ditch that circumnavigated the yard.

Brother Padraig escorted him to the largest roundhouse and gestured for him to enter. Behrt ducked inside the low door, and a hearty voice greeted him. "Come in out of the rain, son."

As Behrt's eyes adjusted to the gloom, he made out a jowly man of middle age, seated at a table lit by a single candle. The vellum leaves of an illuminated codex lay open in front of him, candlelight glinting on the vivid colors.

"I am Abbot Ennae," said the abbot. "Please have a seat." He motioned toward a low stool. He waited politely until Behrt had settled, then folded his hands and leaned forward. "Now tell me what brings you here, my son."

Behrt swallowed hard. He'd had no time to think of a plausible story. He decided to stay as close to the truth as he dared.

"My name is Becc mac Cullen, and I was separated from my party," he said. "I hail from the west coast, and I don't know this part of the country well. I became lost, and wandered for some time, until bandits set upon me on the road. They beat me senseless and took all I had but the clothes on my back. I was very fortunate that they did not kill me, and that I was found by a kind hermit in the forest. Perhaps he was one of yours—Brother Brian?"

The abbot gave him a strange look. "No, he's not from Daire Calgach. But I have heard of Brother Brian."

"I owe him many thanks, for though he had but little, he tended my wounds, fed and housed me until I recovered. But I must have wandered off in a daze, for I woke alone on top of the hill nearby. I don't know how I got there, nor how to find my way back to Brother Brian. I would like to find him and thank him."

The abbot gave him a strange look. "I must tell you that this Brother Brian is not a Christian monk."

"I don't understand," said Behrt. "He wore a habit, threadbare though it was, and he was tonsured..."

"Brian is no Christian. He's a druid. "

The room seemed to tilt for an instant. Behrt stared at the abbot as understanding came over him. "Of course." When the Christian monks first arrived in Ireland, they had adopted the tonsure and robes of the druids to make it easier for the heathen to trust them. Many druids converted and became Christian monks themselves, but some did not. Behrt had heard rumors of a few living as outcasts deep in the forest. He'd always thought them faery tales. Brother Brian must be one of these.

The druid had embodied what Behrt had always believed was the essence of Christian love and charity—but he was a heathen.

Behrt shook off the strangeness that filled him and turned his mind to the concern that burned within—what had become of *Raider Bride,* and Ragnhild? They must have arrived here—what had transpired? Had they attacked? The monastery seemed unscathed. How to find out without giving himself away?

He composed his question carefully. "I've heard that Norse

raiders have been in the area. It appears you have been spared thus far."

Abbot Ennae smiled. "We had a visit from the Norsemen, but no attacks. Our king, Murchad mac Maele Duin, has taken a bride—a *finn gaill.*" The abbot's mouth pinched disapprovingly. "A princess from Lochlainn. She arrived in a fine Norse longship, escorted by her brother and a small fleet of ships. But I am told she refused to become a Christian. It is highly improper for an Irish king to take a heathen for a queen. The marriage was allowed because it formed an alliance to protect us from Norse raiders, but it was not sanctified by the church."

Behrt was glad he was sitting down. His throat tightened as if a strap were cinched around it. *Ragnhild. Married.*

No, betrayed—by her own brother, into the very fate she'd fought so hard to avoid. The abbot said nothing of her shock, of how she must have tried to fight.

Abbot Ennae was staring at him strangely. Behrt struggled to compose his expression into one of idle curiosity. "Where is the royal couple now?"

"The king took his bride to his nearby fortress, Aileach. It was there they were wed. But they are not now in residence. I believe he has taken her to his crannog, deep in the countryside."

Ragnhild was captive, then. Behrt prayed her husband would not harm her. It stood to reason that the man needed her alive to preserve the alliance, but he didn't have to treat her well.

"What became of the rest of the heathen?" he asked casually.

The abbot waved his hand dismissively. "They all departed in their longships as if the devil were after them. And perhaps it was, for King Murchad brought a full military escort to receive his bride. One can't be too careful with the heathens."

When *Raider Bride's* crew saw Ragnhild betrayed, they must have fled. And they'd been pursued no doubt by Harald and Kol. Behrt hoped they'd survived, but they were lost to him now. Once again, he was a man with no people and no country.

A bell tolled and the abbot rose. "It is time for Nones. Will you attend?"

A little stirring of joy rose in Behrt. It had been nearly two years since he'd attended prayer. "I would be very happy to, Father Abbot."

The monastic community gathered in the courtyard around the High Cross. The rain had mercifully stopped and the sun warmed Behrt's head and shoulders. The brothers chanting the familiar psalms in Latin brought a calm he had not felt in a long time. In his borrowed robe, he melded in with the brethren, almost as if he were one of them.

Even after his own clothes had dried, Behrt continued to wear the borrowed habit. It helped him blend in. He was glad that silence was observed most of the time in the monastery. The monks asked him no questions, and they did not think it strange that he volunteered no information about himself.

The simple, routine life of the abbey soothed him—the calls to prayer, the plain meals, the quiet comradery of the brethren as they labored together. Though as a guest he was not expected to work, on his second morning Behrt followed the ring of hammer on iron to the smithy. The scent of the coal fire and tang of hot iron in the air took him back to Ulf's workshop, the one place he'd fit in over the past few years.

The smithy was run by a kindly, elderly monk named Brother Oengus and his young helper, Brother Aidan. Brother Oengus, though still very strong for a man his age, had given the forging over to Brother Aidan. The young monk's forehead glistened with sweat as he smote the glowing iron a tremendous blow. Brother Oengus spent his time creating fine bronze castings for reliquary caskets and book shrines, lighter work that Behrt could participate in. When Behrt shared the fine interlace he'd learned from Ulf, the elder monk eagerly incorporated the designs. For his part, Behrt was happy to be creating works for the glory of God instead of war.

After Behrt had been there a few days, Abbot Ennae called him to his study. "You seem to be making yourself at home here."

Behrt bowed his head. "I am sorry, Father Abbot, I know I have stayed too long. I will take my leave as soon as I can find a place to go."

"Brother Oengus tells me your skills and knowledge of black-smithing technique surpasses his own," said the abbot.

Behrt looked up, stricken. "I meant no disrespect to Brother Oengus."

"You misunderstand me." The abbot was beaming at him. "You have made yourself a useful part of this abbey. I'm asking you if you would like to stay here—make this your home. Perhaps, in time, you will even be moved to take holy orders."

Behrt's heart flared in a moment of hope, then died back just as quickly. These monks would eventually find out about his past, and reject him as everyone else had.

And what of Ragnhild? Would he never see her again?

"It's a big decision. Think about it," said the abbot. "Take your time. You are welcome here for as long as you wish to stay."

Tension flowed from Behrt's shoulders. He had time.

CHAPTER 17

Tullynavin

Ragnhild made herself smile and laugh throughout what had become an impromptu farewell feast. The bard droned on until she wanted to scream, but at last he ceased his wailing and Murchad rose.

Ragnhild followed him to their chamber and returned his kisses, pretending all was well. Before long she didn't have to pretend. As his kisses traveled down her neck, her body responded with a flush of desire. This was the last time he'd ever touch her, and she let her misgivings flow away in the waves of pleasure.

Afterward, she lay in his arms, waiting for him to fall asleep. When his breathing smoothed and lengthened, she extricated herself from his embrace and rose, donned her tunic and breeks and collected her weapons and gear. She stared at his dark shape on the bed, glad his face was lost in shadow, then choked down her regrets and slipped out of the chamber into the night.

She strode across the yard to the cow byre as if she belonged there. Should anyone see her, in the darkness she'd look like any servant boy. When she passed beneath the walls, the night watch didn't spare her a glance.

Her steps slowed as she approached the byre. Holding her breath, she cautiously unlatched the door and edged it open. "Unn! Einar!" she hissed into the darkness. "We must leave now. Bring what food and water you have."

From the depths of the shed came rustles and scrapes as her crew readied themselves. Ragnhild kept watch by the door as they filed out, skirting the byre into the shadow of the wall. When they were all outside, Ragnhild latched the door and crept back to join them. She led the way along the wall to the souterrain's opening.

When the crew had all caught up, she gave them instructions in a whisper. "There are three steps just inside the entrance, and then we enter the cold storage room. At the end of the room is a hole dropping into a long tunnel. Don't worry, it's not very deep. After that there are several more drops, and twists and turns. Just keep following me."

One by one, they stooped into the opening and descended the stone stairs into the souterrain. The room barely held all of them.

When they had all crowded in, Ragnhild bade them collect what provisions they could carry, bundling dried meat and wheels of cheese inside their tunics, tying them tight with the ropes that had been their bonds.

Ragnhild led them to the end of the souterrain. "Here's the first drop," she warned. "Lower yourselves in carefully. The passage gets narrow after this." She eased into the hole, wincing as her raw knees hit the hard rock surface. She gritted her teeth and set off crawling along the stone floor. Behind her she could hear the rasping breath of her crew struggling into the tunnel.

"There's another drop here. The only way in is head first. Let yourselves down easy." She slithered into the hole and squirmed well forward to make room behind her. In spite of her warning, the stone walls echoed with thuds and groans.

"Is everyone all right?" she said.

"I think so," said Einar.

"There's another hole coming up."

More groans, followed by flesh grating on stone and heavy breathing.

"Come on, Alm, move," Einar muttered.

"I can't." There was panic in Alm's whisper.

"You have to keep moving," Ragnhild said, fighting back her own fear. The wounded boy was holding up the entire group, trapping them in the tunnel. "Alm, you can do it. I know you can."

"I've got you," said Einar.

The boy's moans accompanied a scraping sound. "Stop!" he cried. "You're grinding the skin off me."

"Shhh!" Ragnhild hissed.

They all halted.

"Here, put your arms around my waist," said Einar. "Rest your shoulder on my back. I'll haul you along. Can you do that?"

"Yes," the boy quavered. But his whimpers echoed as they struggled down the passageway.

When Ragnhild's forehead hit the stone wall, she greeted the sting with relief. They were nearly at the end.

"The passage makes a sharp left here," she said. "Then a right, a short incline to the entrance, and we come out in the woods."

The air freshened, telling her the exit was near. When she reached the opening, Ragnhild peered through the foliage, scanning their surroundings. Satisfied that they were alone, she shoved into the bushes, forcing her way through the foliage until she spilled out onto the ground with a hard thump. She lay there a moment, gulping in the night air. Then she scrambled to her feet and pulled the shrubbery to one side. Einar came after her, half-carrying Alm. He set the boy on the ground where Alm huddled, stifling his sobs, while Ragnhild helped the rest of the crew clamber out.

"We must get to the boat," she said.

"Give him a moment, for pity's sake," said Unn.

"Get up, lad," said Einar, pulling Alm to his feet. The boy bit back a cry as Einar shouldered him and half-carried, half-dragged him along.

Ragnhild steeled herself to the boy's whimpers as she guided them through the forest toward the boat landing. Where the trees met the riverbank, she gave them a moment to assemble and catch their breath. The moon was shrouded in clouds, but to get to the dock they had to cross a broad expanse of open country without being spotted by the watchmen on the wall and those who guarded the dock.

"Make for the ship!" she whispered, and set out creeping through the brush along the riverbank. Her crew followed single file, heads low, trying their best not to make any noise, but twenty-nine people could not move in complete silence. Einar still supported Alm, and the boy's stifled groans punctuated the rustling of their movements. They flitted between shrubs and clumps of tall grass, pausing to listen and watch for any reactions from the dock or the fort. But there was no sound other than their own labored breath.

Ragnhild halted them in the cover of a copse some distance from the dock, where they crouched in the underbrush, watching the three men who guarded the boats.

She tapped Einar, Thorgeir, and Svein, the most experienced members of the crew. The three húskarlar nodded and broke cover, stealing onto the dock and creeping up behind the guards. Simultaneously, each Norseman grabbed a guard, clapping a hand over their mouths. Before the Irishmen could cry out, the three húskarlar disarmed them and cut their throats with their own knives.

They lowered the corpses silently to the ground and made for

Raider Bride. Ragnhild signaled the rest of the crew and they darted onto the dock, two hefty farm boys all but carrying Alm between them. They scrambled across the Irish boats and onto *Raider Bride.* The boys lowered Alm gently to the deck, where he lay panting. As the last crewmember tumbled aboard, Einar and Thorgeir slashed the mooring lines of the currachs that were rafted to the longship, letting them drift free with the current. Ragnhild cast off *Raider Bride's* lines, and the longship followed the currachs into the stream.

The mast was still stepped and the oars stacked where they'd left them. The Irish had taken away all the valuable weapons, such as axes and swords, but Ragnhild was heartened to see they had left aboard the spears, shields, bows, and quivers of arrows.

Without a sound the crew of *Raider Bride* fitted their oars and began to row against the current. Ragnhild took hold of the tiller and steered them clear of the drifting Irish craft, toward the lough.

Svein stationed himself in the bow, peering into the black night for the withy stakes that marked the passage through the sandbars. He held a white pennant on a stick, which he used to point out the way. Ragnhild steered to the far side of the river, where she hoped the longship would blend into the tree-lined bank.

Still no reaction from the fort. As *Raider Bride* ghosted up the river, Ragnhild stifled the wild laugh that rose in her throat. They were free.

She stared at the fortress. Murchad didn't even know she was gone. He'd wake in the morning to find her place empty and cold.

As they passed the corral, the wind carried a faint whinny to her.

Brunaidh.

Visions of the pony rose in her mind, along with Fergal—even the cursed Fiona. Tears prickled at the corners of her eyes and her throat thickened.

She swallowed hard and focused on her course, watching the moonlight dancing on the water. A dark shape blotted out the moon's reflection—one of the drifting currachs. But they should be behind her, carried downriver on the current that her crew was rowing against.

Ragnhild blinked. The moon popped back out, only to disappear again behind another craft. She heard muffled voices, the splash of a paddle.

She caught her breath as comprehension dawned. A fleet of boats was coming in from the lough, heading their way. Panic seized her for a moment, but then she realized *Raider Bride* could take on any Irish currach. She hissed a warning to Einar, who glanced in the direction she pointed. He nodded, indicating he had seen the currachs. He made his way forward, whispering orders to the crew.

Now that she had spotted them, the boats were easy to see. There were about half a dozen. It would be a brisk battle. As she watched, the huddle of dark craft turned toward shore and beached below the dock. They appeared intent on their destination, unaware of *Raider Bride's* presence on the far side of the river.

What would happen when they found the dead sentries?

The moonlight picked out dozens of figures swarming up the bank toward the fort. They were bypassing the dock entirely. Now she could see them clearly as they ran across the open land that separated the fort from the river.

Where was the tower watch?

As the horde reached the fort, the gate swung open and the dark figures slipped inside.

Treachery.

Inside the fort, lights flared and shouts erupted. Screams split the night as a cloud of black smoke blotted out the stars.

Murchad was in there.

"The fort is under attack!" she said. "I must go back."

"You're crazy," said Einar. "You can't go back there."

Ragnhild set her jaw, steering *Raider Bride* back to the opposite shore. "I'll get off here, and you can take the ship out to sea."

"You can't go alone!"

Ragnhild ran the bow into the riverbank. She grabbed up a spear and shield and vaulted over the side. Her boots sank into the soft mud as she clawed her way up the bank.

"By Loki," said Einar, picking up a spear and shield and climbing over the side after her. "Come on!" The crew of *Raider Bride* armed themselves and splashed ashore behind him, heaving the longship up on the beach.

"Unn, and you three, stay with the wounded, guard the ship," he ordered, pointing at three other crewmembers. "If anyone comes, shove off and drift with the current. We'll catch up with you by land."

They raced across the plain toward the rath. At the open and unguarded gate they gathered in the shadows to catch their breath and assess the situation. Inside, blazing thatch lit the yard like daylight, and the air tasted of smoke. Clusters of men battled each other, their shouts punctuated by screams and the clang of metal.

The Norse crept through the gate, the combatants too involved with each other to notice them.

"Make the swine horn," Ragnhild ordered. They locked their shields, forming a wedge with Ragnhild at the apex, flanked by Einar, Thorgeir, and Svein.

"Charge!" she cried. They surged into the melee, shields locked, spears bristling between them, forging between knots of struggling Irishmen. The combatants whirled to confront this new onslaught, confusion on their faces. The bewildered Irish gave way before the Norse formation as they pierced the epicenter of the battle.

All the while, Ragnhild scanned the crowd for Murchad, but he was nowhere to be seen.

She led the shield wall toward the main hall, where the thatch was already smoldering.

"Murchad!" she rasped, her throat rough from the smoke.

Inside, men shouted in Irish.

"Treachery!" It was Murchad.

"You've betrayed your rightful king." Ragnhild picked out Aed's voice.

"You'll die a traitor's death along with all the Sil nAedo." Ragnhild's blood ran cold.

"Kill them!"

What began as a shriek ended in a gurgle and a thud.

"Into the hall!" she cried and charged the door, her crew locked close to her. She rammed the door with her shoulder, and it buckled under the force of twenty Norse warriors.

They burst inside. The air held an acrid bite of smoke and the floor was littered with dead and dying men. Across the room, a row of spearmen held a cluster of warriors at bay. In their center stood Murchad, shield and sword in hand, flanked by Aed and four others.

"Charge!" Ragnhild cried. The assailants whirled to face the newcomers. Ragnhild did not hesitate, ramming her spear into the throat of the Irishman in front of her and grabbing his axe as he fell. Beside her, Einar drove his own spear into another's guts and claimed his opponent's sword. *Raider Bride's* crew attacked, snatching axes and seaxes from the vanquished, while Murchad and his men fell on their assailants from behind, trapping them between the two groups.

None of the Irish wore armor, nor did the Norse, and very soon the smoky air filled with a mist of blood that spattered the combatants and rained on the floor. The room stank like a butcher's yard. Ragnhild stepped over a corpse and slipped in a pool of gore. She turned her fall into a wild axe swing at an Irishman's chest. He caught her blow on his shield, and she braced herself on the haft of the buried axe to regain her balance. She wrenched the axe from his shield and swung it at his unprotected head. His shriek was cut short and he sagged away, enabling her to jerk the axehead free of his skull and turn on the next man who stood between her and Murchad. His eyes went wide and he leaped out of her way as she charged past.

Murchad's eyes glowed with recognition in his soot- and blood-stained face. He cracked a grin. "*A chroi*, you fight well!"

"We have to go!" shouted Einar.

Ragnhild grabbed Murchad's arm and pulled him toward her crew. Murchad's men joined the Norse to form a shield wall around the Irish king. They charged toward the door, knocking the opposition out of the way.

In the courtyard, Ragnhild squinted across the corpse-strewn ground. The open gate was clogged with men in combat. She glanced toward the souterrain, but there were multiple skirmishes taking place around it. Trying to get her entire crew into the hole one by one was not an option.

"We'll have to charge the gate," she said. Murchad nodded and translated for the Irish. On Ragnhild's signal, her crew shouldered through the doorway in a tight swine array. Murchad loped at her side, followed by Aed and his men. As they crossed the yard, Aed called out to others who dashed from their skirmishes to join them. By the time they drove into the melee at the gate, their number had grown to more than forty.

As Ragnhild led her vanguard through the battle, the Irish rear shields closed ranks, creating a reverse wedge as they backed out through the gate.

"After them!" Ragnhild heard the cry in Irish.

"Run!" she shouted. Outside the gate, the swine horn broke apart and they all ran as fast as they could. "Make for the ship!"

Ragnhild heard the pounding feet and shouts of the enemy behind them. Murchad was beside her, sword in hand, matching her stride, while the Irishmen turned on their pursuers to fight a rear guard. They fell on their enemies with a great roar and clashing of swords on shields.

When Murchad turned back to join Aed, Ragnhild grabbed his arm and yanked him along. "Help me," she said to Einar as Murchad struggled in her grip. The húskarl took hold of Murchad's sword arm and helped her drag him toward the ship.

The Norse didn't look back as they raced across the open ground to the river where *Raider Bride* waited. They slid down the muddy bank and shoved the longship off the beach, then vaulted over the side. Thorgeir took hold of Murchad by his leather jerkin and helped Einar wrestle him aboard.

"I must go back," Murchad cried, struggling in Thorgeir's grip. Massive as the Norseman was, it was all he could do to keep the Irish king from leaping over the side.

"Don't be a fool," said Ragnhild. "You're not going back there." She turned to Thorgeir. "Bind him."

Before Murchad could react, Thorgeir wrested the Irishman's sword from his grip while Svein bound his hands in front of him, then lashed his bonds to the shield rail.

As the current swept them south, Ragnhild took hold of the tiller and aimed the bow toward the lough entrance while the crew fitted their oars and began to row.

Shouts echoed behind them. A few spears whickered over-head, but on the shore Aed's men kept the attackers engaged.

By the glow in the east, dawn was upon them. Beside her, Murchad watched the battle, his lips pressed tight.

"Who were the attackers?" Ragnhild said.

"Conchobar's men. He's discovered that Aed and Diarmait have come over to my side and sent his henchmen to slaughter them. Finding me there was an unexpected windfall. I fear Aed's loyalty to me may cost his people their lives. We must go back."

"There's nothing you can do back there except get yourself killed," said Ragnhild. "Even if we could help them, Aed imprisoned my crew, starved and enslaved them, and would have killed them if he'd had the time. I won't put them back in his power."

"Put me ashore!" Murchad demanded.

Ragnhild's fury rose. "You're on my ship. I give the orders."

Murchad glared at her. "What do you intend to do with me, *a chroi?*" He spat the endearment.

Ragnhild ignored the catch in her stomach. "You made me your prisoner. Now you're mine."

Murchad stared at her in silent shock. She turned away, concentrating on minding the ship's course as her crew rowed against the current that would have swept them back to the fort.

The sounds of slaughter faded behind them. They rounded the bend into the Lough Feabhail where the tide hurried them south.

A flotilla of currachs spilled out of the estuary. The small craft were no match for the longship, but their archers sent up a flight of arrows.

"Row!" cried Ragnhild as she steered *Raider Bride* out of range, the volley streaking into the water a few yards short.

"Are they trying to kill you, or free you?" Ragnhild asked Murchad.

"At this distance, I cannot tell who they are," he replied, his deep voice bitter.

The currachs were still in pursuit, sending another volley. The thuds of arrowheads striking the stern told her they were within range. Regardless of their intent, she had to stop them.

"Archers," she said quietly. Crewmembers stopped rowing and picked up their bows. As the Irish fleet neared, *Raider Bride's* archers nocked and drew, training on the closing enemy.

Ragnhild cried, "Fire!" and they loosed a volley into the currachs. The Irish saw the flight of arrows and dropped their paddles, seizing their shields. The arrows thwacked into enemy fleet, but there were no screams from the Irishmen as the current carried them inexorably down on *Raider Bride.*

CHAPTER 18

Lough Feabhail

The Irish boats swarmed the longship like baitfish. Though bigger than the boats used on the lough, these seagoing currachs were still less than half the length of *Raider Bride,* but there were seven or eight of them--it was hard to tell just how many. If each was manned by half a dozen warriors, they far outnumbered *Raider Bride's* crew.

Ragnhild made her way to Murchad, who was still tied to the shield rail.

"Is this a rescue party or an assassination attempt?" she demanded.

"They're Conchobar's men," he said bitterly. "Untie me and let me fight them."

There was no time to consider. She couldn't leave him helpless for his enemies. If he betrayed her, so be it. She slashed his bonds and turned to join the fight.

Grunts and cries mingled with the clash of weapons. *Raider*

Bride's crew crowded the rails, fending off the Irishmen who threw grappling hooks from both sides. The combatants jabbed spears at each other across the shields that lined *Raider Bride's* gunnels. The longship provided a stable platform on which to fight, while the overloaded currachs rocked dramatically, forcing the Irishmen to jockey as they fought to keep their footing.

There was only room along the rails for a limited number of attackers, enabling the Norse to hold their own at first, but the Irish boats teemed with warriors. For every one that fell, more surged the rails.

Murchad thrust his sword into the Irish mob with vigor, taking a toll on Conchobar's men. Thorgeir, Svein, and Einar had stationed themselves between the less experienced crewmembers, and their axes cut great swathes among the enemy.

The bodies piled up along the sides of the currachs, forcing the Irishmen back from the rails to keep the boats from capsizing. The Norse seized the opportunity to hack with their axes, crushing the currachs' lightweight rails and fragile hulls.

The tide carried the longship south, dragging the crippled Irish craft along. Thorgeir and Einar slashed the grappling lines while Svein and Unn shoved the currachs away with their spears.

As the longship drifted free, the crew took up the oars. While the Irish desperately tried to recover, *Raider Bride* quickly pulled away.

As they rowed south, Ragnhild felt the current slacken against the steering oar. Soon the tide would ebb, turning against them.

She gave the tiller over to Einar and went forward to find Murchad. The Irish king stood by the ship's side, sword still clutched in his hand.

He glared at her. "You don't have to tie me."

"How do I know you won't jump overboard and run?" Ragnhild said. He was in his own country, terrain he knew well. He could easily escape and make his way on foot.

"I give you my word."

Ragnhild crossed her arms over her chest. "I've seen the worth of an Irishman's word."

Murchad caught her gaze and held it. "I give you my word as your husband. I know I owe you my life twice over. I won't try to escape." His eyes were wide and green and guileless.

She hesitated. He was so clever with words. She strained to discern any hidden meaning in them. Murchad said, "*A ghra*, my fortress of Aileach—we can reach it. With the wind and current carrying us at this speed, we should be there in a few hours."

Ragnhild weighed her options. She could try to fight her way north, against the current, through the enemy, back to the open sea. That plan had very little chance of success. More likely she and her crew would be slaughtered by the Irish, and Murchad would die with them. To go south, with the current, carried them away from the enemy, but deeper into the countryside. Murchad's country.

She didn't want to give up her dream of raising an army and beating Harald. The desire for vengeance beat strong in her breast, and for that she needed silver. She had no doubt Murchad kept treasure at Aileach. But to get it, she needed his cooperation.

"Great wrong has been done to me," she said, softening her voice into a reasoning tone. "My brother betrayed me, sold me to you like a slave, all to disinherit me. While you kept me prisoner, he's claimed my land. I intend to set that right. I'll not harm you, but I will take back what's mine. I hope you can understand that."

"I do," he said. "But you must also understand, when I took you to wife it was to form an alliance with your brother to protect my people from Norse attack. I meant no harm to you."

"I realize that," she replied. "But harm me you did. You've deprived me of my freedom, and prevented me from claiming my lands. I will fight my brother to take back my inheritance. When I beat him, I will be supreme in Lochlainn. Your treaty will be with me, and your people will have nothing to fear from the Norse. But to do this, I must raise an army. That takes silver. If you pay me a ransom, I'll set you free and sail for home."

Murchad studied her. She met his gaze, forcing herself to remain still under his scrutiny. Was that disappointment on his face?

He shrugged. "I see I have no choice in the matter. Very well, it shall be as you say." He jutted his chin to the west. "Take me to Aileach and I will give you silver."

Ragnhild eyed her wily husband. He had agreed so easily. Could she trust him?

About as much as he could trust her.

What choice did she have? The Irish fleet were not that far behind them. They would recover in time and attack again.

"There are sandbars ahead, and the tide is turning against us," said Ragnhild. "The Irish boats are lighter than we are, and draw less water. They can float where we cannot. If we go aground now, they'll catch us for sure. We'd be sitting ducks until the next flood."

"Conchobar's men don't know these waters, but I do," said Murchad. "That gives us an advantage. There is a tributary up ahead that will take us close to Aileach. I can guide you there without grounding. From there I can lead you on foot to the fortress."

Ragnhild exhaled. "We have no choice but to try."

"Leave me on the bow and I'll guide you through the sand-bars," said Murchad.

Ragnhild studied him for a moment, her thoughts in turmoil. She was taking a chance. She beckoned Thorgeir. "Give him the pennant. If he tries to escape, kill him."

Thorgeir drew his knife, baring his teeth in a predatory grin.

Murchad said nothing, only leaned over the bow to peer into the water. Ragnhild went aft and took the helm from Einar.

"Left! Bear left," Murchad shouted, flailing the signal flag.

Ragnhild yanked the tiller hard over, hoping her correction

was in time. She cringed as the keel grated. *Raider Bride* shuddered and slowed.

"Row," she barked. The oarsmen put their shoulders into their work, and the ship slithered off the sandbar. Ragnhild breathed again.

"That was too close," she shouted, wiping the prickling sweat from her upper lip.

"I'm trying, *a mhuirin,*" Murchad called. "I have as much to lose as you if they catch us."

Mouthing prayers to the sea goddess, Ragnhild steered blind through the treacherous sands, following Murchad's hand signals. Twice more the keel grated on the bottom, but the rowers managed to propel the longship off the sand.

"Not far," he said. "The river mouth is just up ahead. It's navigable for a ways inland. We'll get fairly close to Aileach before we run out of water. Good cover from the trees there. We'll leave your ship under guard. I'll guide you across the bog to Aileach to claim your ransom. You may leave me there and make your way back to the sea."

It sounded very simple, but Ragnhild had an anxious feeling in the pit of her stomach. Nothing was ever easy.

CHAPTER 19

Daire Calgach Monastery

From the platform inside the monastery walls, Behrt watched the Irish boats arrive.

"Conchobar's men," said the abbot, fear evident in his voice as they watched the warriors beach their currachs and set up camp at the foot of the hill. "He is Murchad's enemy, and does not wish us well. If Conchobar's forces are massing here, they are undoubtedly planning to attack Murchad's fortress, Aileach, a few miles inland. Daire Calgach stands between Conchobar's men and the causeway that leads across the swamps to Aileach. This puts us squarely in harm's way."

Behrt was well aware that Irish kings attacked and looted their rivals' monasteries with impunity. Daire Calgach was Murchad's protectorate—fair game for Conchobar mac Donnchada.

If Ragnhild was at Aileach with her husband, she was in danger.

Behrt's mind raced. What could he do to help the situation? He had no weapons, indeed, the monastery had no arms, only hoes and scythes and wood-axes, butcher knives and a few hunting bows. He doubted any of the brethren had battle experience. And he himself was in no condition to fight.

The abbot called a young monk to him. He wrote a hurried message, sealed it, and gave it to him. "Go out through the back gate," he said. "Take one of the horses and ride as fast as you can to the fortress of Aileach. Tell them we are under attack."

THE TRIBUTARY SNAKED through the countryside, murmuring over stones and eddies. It was a tidal waterway like the Feabhail, with treacherous shallows when the tide was ebbing. But as Murchad had promised, they were able to get a fair distance upriver before they grounded for good. As the river narrowed and shallowed, Murchad guided them into a creek just big enough for *Raider Bride* to enter. Its banks were choked with thick undergrowth that provided excellent cover to hide the longship's low hull.

"You can leave your ship here safely. There is nothing but marsh for miles, and only the locals venture here to hunt," he said. "Get ready for a morning's march across the bogland to Aileach."

With a pang, Ragnhild noticed that Murchad had stopped using the terms of endearment when he addressed her. Her regret was countered by a wave of relief that he was no longer trying to coax her. She felt as if she could trust him more.

"Thorgeir," she said, "you remain behind to guard the ship and the wounded. Choose the men to stay with you."

"Gladly, Lady." Thorgeir named two able-bodied farm boys and Unn, who would care for the wounded.

"Are you certain that will be enough?" she asked.

"If it's not, there's no number that you could leave behind that would be safe," Thorgeir replied. "You need to take a strong force with you."

A chill ran up Ragnhild's spine at his implication of the trouble that lay ahead. She surveyed the twenty who would come across country with her and Murchad—Einar, Svein, and five experienced warriors, as well as Unn's three sisters and ten other women. Though the women were still fairly inexperienced, at least all of them now had been battle-tested. Thorgeir had left her the best fighting force possible.

They packed a day's ration of food and water, and armed themselves with spears, axes, and shields, leaving the rest of the weaponry for the defenders.

Murchad squinted at the horizon, beginning to glow with the dawn. "We should be there by midmorning." Now that he was back on his own land, his vigor seemed to return. He strode into the marsh confidently, smiling up at the sky while whistling a jaunty tune. At first he followed what appeared to be a game trail through the wetlands, but soon he branched off across a trackless water meadow, slogging from copse to copse.

Ragnhild worried that he led them through such treacherous country. It would be so easy to step off into the pervasive boglands and sink—up to their knees, or deeper yet. She shuddered. They were at Murchad's mercy once again, no matter that they outnumbered him. And once they reached the fortress, they would lose their advantage in numbers.

She tried to keep track of the landmarks as they went. "Do you think you can find your way back on your own?" she muttered to Einar.

"Maybe," he said cautiously. "There are a lot of course changes to remember, and so many stretches of bog without a trail."

Uneasiness gnawed at her. They wouldn't enter the fortress, they'd hold Murchad outside the gates until the silver was paid. That part should go easily enough. He'd promised her the ransom, and he'd never broken his word to her. The critical part would be when they released him—without Murchad as hostage, they might have to fight their way out. And if they had to find their way back to the ship on their own—she feared they would become hopelessly lost in the endless wetlands. Perhaps Murchad was counting on that.

She would have to keep him prisoner and compel him to guide them back to the ship. But there was still the chance that he'd lead them to their deaths, stranding them in the swamp.

As Murchad had promised, by midmorning their track solidified into a road and they sighted the fortress in the distance. Hoofbeats sounded and horsemen appeared.

"Ready yourselves," Ragnhild murmured to her party as a dozen mounted warriors rode down on them. She drew her hunting knife and took a firm grip on Murchad while the Norse formed a shield wall around them, protecting all sides.

The horsemen encircled them.

"My lord," their leader exclaimed, staring down at Murchad in the midst of the Norse. "I am so happy to see you! We thought you dead."

"Very much alive, Cerball," said Murchad cheerfully as Ragnhild pressed the point of her knife to his kidney. "Thanks to my wife, and her crew of *finn gaill*. And to brave Aed. Has there been any news of him? Or of Tullynavin?"

"Tullynavin burned," said Cerball grimly. "Aed survived, but he was gravely wounded."

"May God keep him," said Murchad. The Irish crossed themselves. "Please escort us into the fortress. I have a matter I must resolve with my wife."

"Of course, my lord." Cerball gave a hand signal and two horsemen dismounted, offering their horses to Murchad and Ragnhild.

Ragnhild shook her head, keeping a tight grip on Murchad. "My husband and I will remain with my guard," she said in Irish.

Cerball shot her an aggressive look. Ragnhild dug her blade into Murchad's back.

"We will do as the lady wishes," said Murchad.

"As you say, my lord," said Cerball, the note of defiance still in his voice.

The Irish escorted them to the gate, the Norse warriors maintaining their tight formation around Murchad and Ragnhild.

As they neared the fortress, Ragnhild stared up at the men lining the palisade and its watchtower. If they went inside, they'd never come out.

"You may leave us," she said to Cerball. "We will wait here until our matter is resolved."

In spite of the long knife pressing on his kidney, Murchad gave her a delighted grin. "You give orders like a true Irish queen!"

Ragnhild gave him a tight smile.

"Do as your queen commands," Murchad said to Cerball. "Send Father Ferdia to me."

"Yes, my lord." Cerball whistled and the gates opened.

Ragnhild gave her husband a stern look. "Why are you calling a priest? I want the ransom, and my sword."

"And you shall have them both, wife. Father Ferdia is the only other person I trust to give access to the treasury."

"Very well. Once the ransom is paid, you must escort us safely back to my ship. Then you will be free to go."

"As you command," said Murchad. For the first time, his smile collapsed, replaced with a solemn expression. Ragnhild hardened her heart to it and turned her attention to their present situation.

The Norse strengthened their formation beneath the watch tower's scrutiny. *Raider Bride's* crewmembers spelled each other, holding their shields overhead for protection against the glaring sun as well as any missiles from the tower watch, while the others rested their arms, shields pulled in close to their bodies.

They could only keep their defenses up so long. Ragnhild wanted to be off before anything could go wrong.

Murchad alone seemed at ease in his predicament. Ragnhild had removed her knife from his kidneys, but she kept a firm grip on his arm.

At last the gates creaked open and Father Ferdia emerged, followed by Murchad's cousin, Niall, and thirty armed men. Ragnhild tensed. Niall wore Lady's Servant on his belt.

He shouted in a voice like thunder. "We will take these *finn gaill* prisoner."

The Irish men-at-arms surrounded them, weapons drawn. On the top of the wall, more warriors stood ready, bristling with arrows and spears.

"They are the household guard of your queen and under my protection," Murchad said heatedly.

Father Ferdia interrupted. "No heathen can be a queen in Ireland, and it is unfitting for a king of Aileach to be wed to such a creature. I insist that you renounce this woman and turn her and her rabble over to the guards."

Murchad glared at his cousin and the priest, a dangerous glint in his eye. "Are you challenging me?"

Father Ferdia and Niall exchanged glances. Niall took a deep breath and stepped forward. "We feared you were dead, cousin."

Murchad's face went pale, his expression thunderstruck. "You've called the brehons?"

"I have," said Niall. "When you were declared dead, they made their ruling and the men of Cenel nEoghan have voted."

Murchad shot his cousin a bitter look. "I suppose they have elected you to take my place."

Niall nodded.

"Well, I stand before you, very much alive, and I'm here to take my kingship back," Murchad declared.

Father Ferdia glowered. "It was bad enough that you constantly called the men of the Cenel nEoghan to make war against the Ard Ri, dragging them from their farm work and wasting their lives in a vain pursuit. Now you have wed a heathen and, worse, you take her side against your countrymen."

"I have done what is best for Ireland," Murchad said.

"Your behavior is unbefitting a king of Aileach," Father Ferdia bellowed. "If you won't renounce this unholy marriage, your cousin will remain king."

"I'll not renounce my wife nor her people," said Murchad harshly. "There are men who will still swear to me."

"This I know, cousin," Niall said, his bluster faltering. "If you choose to resist, much blood will be shed among our kinsmen. You've been my brother all my life, and I've always looked up to you. It was you who avenged my father's murder. I never wanted it to come to this. But you know as well as I that since my father was the last Ard Ri, it is the right of the Southern Ui Neill to take the High Kingship in their turn. You must give up your cause and recognize Conchobar as Ard Ri."

Ragnhild stared at her husband. In spite of what he'd told her, it was he who'd stolen the High Kingship—not Conchobar.

"But I'm the better man!" Murchad said. "Conchobar is not fit to be king."

"I don't disagree with you, cousin," Niall said. "But our families have honored this agreement since ancient times. We must uphold it now." He turned his stern gaze on Ragnhild. "And even if you accept Conchobar as the Ard Ri, you must renounce this heathen. If you do not, we'll call the brehons, and let them decide who should be king of Aileach. They are unlikely to rule in your favor."

Murchad stared at his cousin. Ragnhild held her breath while she kept a stone face. She knew how much his kingship and his people meant to Murchad. He only had one choice, really, and that was to divorce her and turn her crew over to Niall. No matter what Murchad said, the Irish warriors would take them by force soon enough. She tightened her grip on her knife. They would die fighting someday, and today was as good as any.

Murchad took a deep breath and eyed his cousin sadly. "If you promise to let my wife and her house guard go free, I will abdicate my kingship willingly and trouble you no more."

Ragnhild could not believe what she'd heard.

Niall shook his head in disbelief. "Does this heathen mean so much to you? That you would give up everything?"

Murchad gazed at Ragnhild. "She does—for her at least I can trust. She is like the Irish queens of ancient times, bold and commanding. I would not be happy without her." He bowed to her. "Lady, will you have a common man for a husband?"

Ragnhild's eyes widened. Though a bubble of joy rose up inside her, she couldn't let him have it all his own way. "I had never planned on a husband, king or no," she said in Irish.

She watched Murchad's confident expression collapse, and a strange tender spot opened up in her chest, like an unhealed wound. She sighed. Was she never to be rid of lovesick men? "I suppose I will take you after all."

The relief that flooded his features made the tender spot swell.

Murchad turned back to Niall. "Cousin, I have one more condition. You must return my wife's sword."

With a sour expression, Niall slid Lady's Servant from the scabbard and held it out, hilt-first, to Murchad.

Ragnhild tossed her knife to her left hand and snatched the sword from Niall's grip in one smooth motion. The Irishman gaped at her as she brandished a blade in each hand, grinning.

Murchad took hold of the golden torc around his neck and pried it apart. He held it out to Niall with a bow and a flourish. "Hail to thee, Niall mac Aeda, King of Aileach." He turned to Ragnhild. "I am sorry I can't fulfill the rest of my promise to you. I no longer have rights to the treasury of Aileach."

Ragnhild thought of Brisingamen, nestled golden and

gleaming in the bottom of her sea chest, and a slow smile spread across her face. "Never mind. Let's be off." *Before your cousin changes his mind.*

As *Raider Bride's* crew lowered their shields and reassembled for the return journey, a young monk on horseback came pelting up the roadway. He pulled up his lathered horse and gasped, "Conchobar's men are attacking Daire Calgach!"

Niall missed no more than a heartbeat before turning to the men on the wall and shouting, "Rally our forces."

Murchad turned a stricken face to Ragnhild. "I must join them," he said.

"After what they've done to you?"

"They are my people. I will defend them as long as I draw breath."

Ragnhild felt as if she'd been gut-punched. She would be going back without him, after all. She knew she'd make the same choice. "Do what you must. But first you need to lead us back to the ship. We'll drop you on shore near the causeway where you can join Niall."

Murchad looked apprehensive. She'd given him no reason to trust her.

"You gave your word," she reminded him. "I swear to Freyja that I will set you free once we are back on *Raider Bride.*"

Murchad's expression told her he didn't completely believe her. "Very well."

While Niall rallied his men, the Norse turned their backs on Aileach. Murchad led them through the marsh and forest in silence. Ragnhild wanted to say something comforting, but the stern set of his shoulders forbade sympathy. He was a king deposed—the ultimate humiliation. She wondered how he could bear it. But Murchad was a different kind of man than she had ever met before. Something told her he'd recover from the injury to his pride.

I'll be free. He can join his battle, and I'll just sail away. I still have

Brisingamen. That necklace has a lot of gold in it. Maybe enough to fund my war on Harald.

But as she imagined his wiry frame dwindling in the distance, her high spirits collapsed. There was nobody like him. Nobody with green eyes that danced when they looked at her. Nobody with that laugh, that special lilt to his Norse.

And she would never see Fergal again, or Brunaidh. The loss of the pony especially hurt. She would even miss Fiona. The Irishwoman had treated her lover's wife with undeserved kindness. Well, Fiona would have Murchad all to herself, soon enough.

She wrenched her thoughts away from that path and forced them to the future. Once she had sailed home, how would she go after Harald? His position in their father's port was strong, nearly impregnable. It was impossible to approach by sea without being seen. She could come around from the south, from Tromøy, land *Raider Bride* in a hidden cove and attack overland as she had when she raided her father's hoard the year before. But that had been only a small contingent, and they had not approached the settlement itself. It seemed unlikely that she could march a large enough army to overcome him cross country without being detected. Lacking the advantage of surprise, she'd have to bring an overwhelming force regardless of whether she attacked by land or sea. Where would she get the warriors? Åsa, beset as she was by hostile neighbors, could only afford to supply a small portion of her own troops. Olaf would no doubt contribute a few, but it wouldn't be enough to take on Harald.

She'd have to recruit new warriors at the fall assembly, and train them over the winter. Åsa would be willing to accommodate the new forces, but Ragnhild would have to find a way to supply extra provisions to feed them.

Harald was probably already home, snug in Father's hall. He wouldn't know she'd escaped her marriage. But when she appeared at the assembly to recruit more warriors, he'd be forewarned. How to keep her presence a secret? Perhaps Åsa would agree to recruit on her behalf?

Raider Bride's mast appeared above the trees, ending her reverie. Ragnhild called out, and Unn appeared from the dense foliage and led them to the ship.

Thorgeir raised his eyebrows when Murchad came aboard with a face like thunder. Ragnhild shook her head in warning and the crew kept silent.

"We need to depart immediately," she ordered. "We will be taking Murchad to join his forces—there is an attack on the monastery."

Raider Bride's crew scurried to get underway. They grabbed hold of the branches to haul the ship out of the creek. Once in the tributary, they fitted their oars, rowing against the flood tide toward the Feabhail. Murchad stayed in the bow, directing Ragnhild around sandbars and snags. Steering absorbed all of her concentration.

Long before they reached the confluence of the rivers, she felt the mighty Feabhail in the quiver of the steering board. Passing through a thick copse of trees, the waterway made a sharp bend and the current swept *Raider Bride* onto the river. The flood tide hurried them south, at a fast enough clip that the rowers could rest their oars.

The river narrowed and curved, fraught with back currents and tide rips. Murchad remained on the bow while Ragnhild kept hold of the tiller. She knew she could trust any of the three húskarlar to bring them through the treacherous waters, but she needed to keep her mind engaged.

The afternoon light picked out a sleek shape slicing through the water ahead of them, heading upriver. Squinting at it, Ragnhild was able to make out the line of a slender, curving hull, a high prow. A Norse longship, headed toward Daire Calgach. So much for Harald's promise to keep his countrymen from attacking.

Fingers to her lips, she tapped Einar's shoulder, pointing at the ship. He drew a sharp intake of breath.

She steered *Raider Bride* close to the opposite shore as they followed the other ship, flowing silently along with the current, their low hull blending into the shoreline.

As Ragnhild stared at their quarry, she picked out the shape of the prow beast.

A swan.

Battle Swan.

It was Harald's ship.

CHAPTER 20

Murchad raced back from the bow. Ragnhild held a finger to her lips. Her heart thundered as she watched the longship land on the shore beneath the monastery walls.

Einar murmured, "That's Harald."

Ragnhild nodded. "Reneging on his bargain."

"An oath-breaker," said Murchad bitterly.

Ragnhild smiled. "While he's busy breaking his oath, we can attack him from behind."

Murchad flashed a grin. She was glad to see him smile. "I thought you were going to put me ashore to meet up with Niall, and sail away?"

Ragnhild scanned the river. "There's no sign of Kol's ships. The Orcadians must have returned home. This is our best opportunity to take Harald."

She could make out dark shapes of warriors already swarming the hillside. Harald's crew vaulted into the water and unloaded something large and heavy from *Battle Swan*. Half as long as the ship's hull and as big around as a man, it appeared to be a tree trunk. As she watched them float it ashore, Ragnhild realized what it was.

A battering ram.

Ragnhild eyed Daire Calgach's gate. Though made of oak, it was flimsy compared to the massive log Harald's warriors floated to the beach.

Battle Swan's crew joined Conchobar's men on the shore, the two parties forming a group of close to eighty warriors. A dozen of Harald's men took up the huge log while the others massed around them, and the whole party advanced on the monastery's gate. Defenders appeared on the walls, sending out a few arrows, but not enough to slow the attackers' inexorable pace.

Ragnhild put the helm over and closed the beach while *Raider Bride's* crew armed themselves.

As she had hoped, there were no lookouts posted. Harald would not expect an attack from the river. The enemy was focused on their assault on the monastery, and failed to notice *Raider Bride's* approach. Perhaps the Irish thought they were one of Harald's fleet. Ragnhild's heart drummed as the ship glided in alongside *Battle Swan.* Her crew slipped over the side without a sound.

They gathered on the beach, forming a shield wall. "Hold a moment," Ragnhild whispered. With a wicked grin she jerked her head toward *Battle Swan.* "I know where Harald keeps his treasure."

She slipped aboard her brother's ship, followed by Thorgeir. She went to the stern and pulled up a loose plank. The big warrior helped her drag the oaken chest from the longship's hold and passed it over the side to Einar and Svein, who stowed the chest beneath *Raider Bride's* floorboards.

They took their places in the shield wall, and when their formation was tight, Ragnhild raised her arm and motioned them forward.

They sprinted up the beach, their footfalls muted by the sand. The first Harald's warriors knew anything was amiss was when they died with a spear in their backs. The screams of the men in the rearguard distracted those lugging the battering ram while the defenders on the walls rained arrows and rocks down on them.

Ragnhild held her people back while the missiles took their toll on Harald's men. When the steel rain stopped falling, she signaled the shield wall forward. *Raider Bride's* crew screamed a battle cry as they bore down on the raiders.

BEHRT WATCHED from Daire's walls. Harald's men lugged the battering ram toward the gate while Conchobar's men swarmed around them. Conchobar's party, which had started out as nearly forty men, now augmented by Harald's crew of thirty-five.

There were close to one hundred men within Daire Calgach's walls, but the monks were untrained in fighting; indeed, few of them even had hunting experience. Those that knew how to shoot a bow positioned themselves on the platform that ran inside the wall, interspersed among the other brethren who flung rocks that rarely hit their mark. Their efforts barely slowed the attackers down.

As the battering ram came within range Behrt drew his bow and held, steeling the quiver in his gut. He was amazed that he could do it, and found himself wondering if there was more to Brother Brian's healing than he knew. Falling back on years of training, he tapped a deep well of strength within. He would defend this place or die in the attempt.

He loosed just as the leader of the ram-bearers made the mistake of looking up at him. Behrt's arrow pierced the man's throat and he fell. The warrior behind him stumbled over his corpse and the heavy log swayed, but the man kept his feet and another stepped in line to take the dead man's place.

Arrows flew from Conchobar's men, but the monastery's wall provided the monks with good cover. Behrt dodged a missile as he nocked another arrow and loosed, hitting the new lead ram-bearer squarely in the chest. This warrior wore a leather jerkin and Behrt's arrow lodged there, but the man staggered on, half-propped by the others.

Behrt ignored the sharp pain that lanced through his middle as he drew again. The arrow quivered on the string. His old wounds had been taxed beyond their limits. He let fly before he lost all control, but the arrow went wild, passing over the heads of the enemy.

He turned to Brother Aidan, who stood behind him. "It's up to you now," he said, handing his bow to the young monk.

Brother Aidan took the weapon cautiously. His work in the smithy had given him impressive upper-body strength, but he'd had no training.

"Take a firm grip," Behrt instructed. "Like this." He placed Aidan's hands on the bow and plucked an arrow from his quiver, nocking the fletched end on the string. "Pull back and hold." He placed his hand over the younger man's, guiding his arm as they pulled the arrow back. "Take aim at that one's chest," he said, sighting over Aidan's shoulder. "Now loose." The arrow shot from the bow. It flew straight into the chest of the battering ram's leader, knocking him back a pace and sticking next to Behrt's arrow.

Brother Aidan flashed Behrt a look of delight.

"You're a natural," said Behrt. "Let's try again." The young monk eagerly fitted another arrow. Behrt guided his aim but let the younger man's strength bend the bow and draw the arrow. They shot at the same lead man, with two arrows already lodged in his leather jerkin. This time the tip penetrated the leather and the man fell with a cry.

"We got him!" shouted Brother Aidan, then hastily crossed himself.

Behrt smiled. This young monk had the makings of a warrior.

"Remember, we are defending God's house. Now, try it on your own."

While Brother Aidan fitted the arrow, Behrt went to the next brother, a young man who held his bow awkwardly and seemed reluctant to nock his arrow. "Here, grip the bow like this." He guided the monk's shot and picked off another ram-bearer. "Good! Do you think you can manage that again?" The young man nodded vigorously and nocked another arrow. Behrt moved on.

A second longship surged up on the shore. Behrt's stomach dropped. They couldn't fend off another crew.

Then he recognized *Raider Bride*. A shock of relief ran through him. They were alive! His heart soared when he saw Ragnhild leap from the ship. He could never mistake her for any other woman. Behind her came a black-haired man, an Irish warrior by his dress.

But they were attacking the monastery. Had they joined with Harald?

He watched Ragnhild board *Battle Swan*, followed by Thorgeir. They retrieved something heavy and lugged it back aboard *Raider Bride*.

Ragnhild returned to the beach and mustered her crew. Harald and the Irish attackers, intent on the monastery, did not seem to be aware of them as Ragnhild led the charge up the hill. A jolt of fierce joy shot through Behrt as *Raider Bride's* crew fell on the attackers, cutting down a swath of the rear guard.

For the moment, Ragnhild and her people were out of range of Daire's missiles. Behrt hurried to the next monk and helped him draw his bow. "Take care not to hit that rear party," he called. "They're on our side."

SWORD DRAWN, Ragnhild charged up the hill, Murchad by her side. Behind them ran the three húskarlar and every able-bodied member of *Raider Bride's* crew, each one of them lusting for Harald's death.

As they entered the melee, Murchad spotted someone in the crowd and cried, "Fallon, you traitor!" and split off from the crew. In an instant the churning mass swallowed him.

Ragnhild spotted her brother by his leather armor and helm, rallying his men into formation. "There he is," she shouted. Einar's head swiveled to seek out Harald at the center of a tight shield wall.

"Swine array!" cried Ragnhild. Svein brought his shield up with hers while Einar and Thorgeir matched her other side and *Raider Bride's* crew locked in tight behind them. They stormed through the combatants toward Harald's knot of men.

As they closed on her brother, Harald glanced over and met Ragnhild's gaze. Shock flashed across his face before dissolving into a scowl. *Raider Bride's* crew fell on Harald's guard while Ragnhild and Einar drove through his defense. One of Harald's warriors stood in their way, sword drawn, but Svein swung his axe, battering the man to the ground. Einar and Thorgeir engaged a man each, leaving Harald standing alone.

"Hello, brother!" Ragnhild glared up at her brother. He topped her by half a head and outweighed her by fifty pounds.

"I should have known that Irishman couldn't handle you," Harald sneered. "I should have killed you when I had the chance."

"That would make you a kin slayer," said Ragnhild. "Unfit to be king."

"And who's to tell that tale?" Harald snarled, swinging his sword at her.

Ragnhild took the blow on her shield and thrust her blade into the opening. Harald leaped back and struck again, so quickly that Ragnhild could not get her shield up. She managed to pivot and Harald's blade swept by, glancing off her chain mail.

Ragnhild completed the circle and came up on her brother's blind side, slashing her sword into his arm hard enough to make him drop his shield while she bashed her own shield into his helmet. Ragnhild took the opening to ram her sword into her brother's midriff. He dodged back enough that his leather armor stopped the point, but the blow forced the wind from him and he buckled at the waist with a huff. While Ragnhild recovered from the strike, Harald straightened. His eyes bored into hers with insane rage.

He hacked his sword down on her, forcing her to step back.

"Surrender to me, little sister," Harald rasped. "I'll let you live."

Ragnhild moved laterally, making her way around Harald as he pivoted in place, keeping his sword trained on her. Even without a shield, he gave her no opening. She needed to goad him into attacking her.

"You're just a bully," she taunted. "Your reputation is already ruined just by fighting me. I'm going to defeat you. Save yourself the humiliation of being beaten by your little sister. Throw down your sword before I make a fool of you."

Harald laughed and lunged for her. He thrust his sword at her head and she dodged to one side, swinging her own blade. Harald's sword whooshed by her face as hers caught him in the chest, knocking him off balance. This time, he stumbled back and she advanced on him, sword raised for another blow.

"Ragnhild!" She whirled to face an Irishman who bore down on her, Murchad hot on his heels. She ducked away from the attack as Murchad ran him through.

Conchobar's men swarmed around them, separating them from Harald and cutting them off from *Raider Bride's* forces. Ragnhild put her back to Murchad's and they stood firm, shields up and swords leveled as the enemy horde closed in.

"This is how a king and queen are meant to be, *a ghra*," Murchad said. "Fighting together."

Ragnhild felt him behind her, strongly rooted as an oak.

Arrows whickered down from the monastery walls with deadly aim, dropping five attackers. As she impaled a charging warrior, Ragnhild shot a glance up at the wall in time to see Behrt sketch a bow to her. He nocked another arrow, and she jerked her sword free, turning on the next man in line.

Harald's men still lugged the battering ram up the hill, slowed by the continued barrage of missiles from the walls.

They were still a hundred yards away when the monastery gates opened and the mounted troops of Aileach poured forth, Niall at their head. They rode into the attackers, slashing down with their swords, trampling them. Harald's men dropped the battering ram and scattered.

Ragnhild fought her way through the mob that surrounded her, trying to get to her brother. A horn sounded from the shore.

The signal for retreat.

Harald and his men split off from the battle, deserting their Irish allies and running for *Battle Swan*.

Ragnhild hacked wildly at the men between her and Harald, but the battle between Niall's horsemen and Conchobar's forces hemmed her in.

Harald and his crew reached *Battle Swan* and shoved the longship into the water. They leaped aboard and took up their oars, rowing toward the Lough Feabhail and the open sea. Ragnhild ground her teeth in impotent fury.

The battle was winding down as Niall's horsemen rode down Conchobar's remaining Irish. Ragnhild called her crew to fall back into a support position, away from the flailing hooves and slashing swords.

Soon the butchery was done. *Raider Bride's* crew raised a cheer as they helped Niall's forces disarm Conchobar's surviving men, rounding them up and roping them together.

Niall dismounted and faced Murchad, who stood beside Ragnhild, his sword caked in blood.

"I thank you for your aid, cousin," said Niall.

"Thank my wife and her crew. They saved you, in spite of the fact that you wished to take them prisoner."

Niall bowed his head to Ragnhild. "My thanks, Lady. I owe you a great debt."

Ragnhild scowled at him. "We fought for Murchad, not a sorry traitor like you."

Niall turned away as a Christ priest, dressed in splendid robes, led a party of monks out of the monastery gate. He approached Niall and bowed. "I thank you for coming to our rescue, Lord King."

The priest turned to Murchad and bowed low before him. "Lord Murchad," he said, nervously eyeing Ragnhild and her crew. "We thank you for coming to our aid."

"You are most welcome, Father Abbot," said Murchad. "But you owe your thanks to my wife and her crew."

"Of course." The abbot hurriedly bowed to Ragnhild. "Our thanks, my lady," he said in heavily accented Norse. "Please bring your people inside. We will make you comfortable."

Ragnhild was not likely to ever go inside an Irish stronghold again, even a monastery. "Thank you," she said. The abbot's brows shot up at her perfect Irish. "We'll set up camp on the shore and tend to our dead and wounded. We would appreciate some food and ale, bandages and medicines."

A look of relief crossed the abbot's face. "As you will, Lady."

"I will remain with my wife," Murchad said.

Without another word, the abbot turned away and hurried back inside the gates.

Ragnhild busied her crew, setting up camp. Those who were unscathed pitched the awning on the beach and made the wounded comfortable while Ragnhild and Unn assessed the injuries. Though there were plenty of lacerations and broken bones, Ragnhild was grateful that none of them had been killed. Poor Alm had fought bravely, but now his condition was grave. "All we can do is keep him comfortable," Unn said as they wrapped him in furs and fed him an infusion from their store of willow bark.

Ragnhild glimpsed Murchad, sitting by himself, staring out over the water. She put down the linen she was tearing into a bandage and made her way to him.

"You are still my husband," she began, settling herself on the ground beside him.

He didn't respond, just kept his gaze fixed on the water.

"If you return with me to Lochlainn, we can raise an army and claim my land of Gausel. I realize it's not so grand as being king of Aileach."

"Why would you want me with you? I'm a failure."

"You're no failure," she said. "You're a great warrior. And Gausel is situated in a perfect location to keep watch on the sailing route to Ireland. You can keep your vow to protect your people from there."

At last he turned his head to her. "You still want me?"

"I do," said Ragnhild, surprised to realize that she meant it. "As long as I can have you on my own terms, and not as some captive peace-cow."

"Perhaps now I know a little of how you felt," he said.

She reached out and laid a hand on his arm.

He took her hand in his and kissed it. "You are the perfect wife for me." He put his arm around her and pulled her to him. They sat there together, gazing at the sea.

Through the gates of Daire Calgach walked a new party of monks, bearing a cask of ale and two large baskets filled with food. The tall figure who led them halted before Ragnhild and threw back his hood.

It was Behrt.

Behrt approached with a hesitant step, leading his brothers toward Ragnhild and the crew of *Raider Bride*. How would his former shipmates react after he had deserted them, gone off to warn their intended victims? He felt even more of an outsider than ever before, but took some comfort from the monks behind him.

Pain seared through Behrt at the sight of Ragnhild seated beside Murchad. The two of them looked very happy.

"Behrt!" He searched Ragnhild's face for some reaction, but her expression was unreadable.

"Greetings, shield-maiden." Behrt bowed his head. "Please accept these provisions with our thanks."

Silence hung in the air between them. His former shipmates stared at him, inscrutable. He waited.

"You abandoned us," she said flatly.

Behrt looked up to meet her eyes. "I am sorry." His gaze swept the crew. "I apologize to you all. You trusted me and I betrayed you. But I could not stand by and let these defenseless men be slaughtered."

"Not so defenseless," Ragnhild said. "I saw them shooting arrows from the wall."

"I helped them learn to defend themselves."

Ragnhild cleared her throat. "I know you saved my life today, and some others. I thank you for that."

Behrt thought the crew's expressions softened at her words, but he waited in silence.

"Join us," said Ragnhild at last. She turned to Murchad. "Husband, meet our long-lost brother at arms, Behrt. Behrt, this is my husband, Murchad."

"Lord King." Behrt bowed his head to Murchad.

"I am king no longer," said Murchad. "My cousin Niall has deposed me."

"Because he has a heathen for a wife," added Ragnhild. "But

Murchad refused to annul the marriage." Murchad smiled at her, and when she met his gaze the two of them radiated joy.

At that moment, Behrt's decision came clear. He had his answer for Abbot Ennae.

"I heard that you were married," said Behrt. "But I cannot imagine how that came about."

"Harald betrayed me, and sold me to Murchad," Ragnhild said. "At first I was a captive, and thought I would die of it. But after awhile, I got used to my husband." She exchanged a smile with Murchad.

"Now please, Behrt, sit, and tell us all that has befallen you." Ragnhild moved over to make room for him. The rest of the crew gathered around to listen.

Behrt took a seat on the log and helped himself to a cup of ale as he told them his strange saga.

"Brother Brian must have been a land-wight," said Ragnhild.

"He was a druid," said Murchad. "There are still a few of them left, living far from civilization."

"You're dressed as a Christ-priest," Einar said.

"Yes," said Behrt. "I have decided to stay here, and study in preparation to take my vows. I am called Brother Becc now."

"Is that what you want?" said Ragnhild. "You may sail home with us."

At her words, relief surged over him. He had her forgiveness. "I'm sure. This is my home now, and these are my brethren." Behrt gestured to the monks who served food and ale to the crew.

Ragnhild looked searchingly into Behrt's eyes. "We'll miss you." As she uttered the platitude, a look of pain and loss crossed her face, and he realized she meant what she said.

"You may yet see me again," said Behrt with a mysterious smile. "Perhaps one day the Lord will send me on a mission to bring His word to the heathen."

"You will always be welcome in Gausel, once I take it from Harald," said Ragnhild. "Just don't expect to find many converts."

Murchad said, "Who knows when that will be. I am sorry that I could not give you the treasure I promised."

"Fear not, husband," said Ragnhild with a sly smile. "I have wealth enough. But I wonder what Harald will do when he finds my bride-price missing."

Murchad stared at Ragnhild in astonishment that changed to delight when he realized what she meant. The two of them began to laugh, their arms going around each other.

The laughter trailed off, and she looked seriously at Murchad. "Since my brother reneged on his side of the bargain, I took back my bride-price for you."

"It will help us muster an army to secure your kingdom," said Murchad.

"Us?" said Ragnhild, staring at her husband. "Are you sure? Do you truly want to leave your homeland, to live among the heathen?"

"There is nothing for me here," he said. "My home is where you are."

"Åsa will certainly be surprised," said Ragnhild. "I set out to kill a king, and return with a husband."

"You're the last person Åsa would ever expect to bring home a husband," said Unn.

Ragnhild laughed. "What other plunder would you expect *Raider Bride* to bring home?"

AFTERWORD

Thank you for reading! I hope you enjoyed *The Raider Bride*. If you did, a short review would be greatly appreciated. Reviews help other readers find books they love.

Join my mailing list and get a free short story, *Mistress of Magic,* the origin story of the sorceress Heid. This prequel is only available to subscribers on my mailing list.

Sign up to get updates of forthcoming titles in The Norsewomen Series and fascinating facts about the Viking Era.

For details, please visit my website:

https://JohannaWittenberg.com

HISTORICAL NOTE

Ragnhild and the crew of *Raider Bride* find themselves in a strange land of enchantment, with many differences and surprising similarities with Scandinavia.

Murchad mac Maele Duin was a real Irish king, and his rivalry with Conchobar mac Donnchada was fact. Murchad was deposed by his cousin, Niall mac Aeda, who became High King upon Conchobar's death in 833.

Kingship in early medieval Ireland was not by primogeniture. Any man of high enough birth was eligible to be elected king of his tuath, or of larger areas. The Ui Neill clan claimed the High Kingship during this time, though the idea of the Ard Ri—High King—of all Ireland was apparently more of a concept than a reality, for never did all the warring factions unite under one king. In this way Ireland was much like Norway of the time, made up of dozens of warring petty kingdoms.

Women in early medieval Ireland had nearly equal rights with their Scandinavian counterparts. Like Norway, Ireland was never conquered by the Romans and though they adopted Christianity early on, the Celtic Church was kept separate from secular matters such as marriage. Irishwomen could own property, and their consent was required in marriage. Husbands could not enter into contracts without their principal wife's consent. There were numerous types of marriages recognized under gaelic (brehon) law—"first" or principal marriages between a couple of equal rank, further subdivided depending on who brought the most wealth to the marriage, on down through various levels of concubinage and even non-consensual sex, which enabled the illegitimate offspring rights of inheritance. Trial marriages (hand-fasting) and divorce were allowed.

Druids, brehons, and bards were high-ranking members of the filidh, the intellectual class of ancient Irish society. Their origins are lost in the mists of time, though they were known to the Romans. Their ranks were attained through years of study. Both men and women could become members of the filidh. At some point a student would choose a branch to specialize in, whether as judges (brehons), historians, bards, or druids. Further, there were ranks within the specialties, such as Ollave, the highest rank of the bardic branch—requiring twelve years of study. After Ireland converted to Christianity in the fifth century, many druids became Christian monks and nuns, continuing their studies as before. But brehons and bards continued in their secular roles up until the British conquest of the 1600s.

There has been much discussion as to whether the royal fortress of Aileach was located at the Grianan, an ancient hillfort atop Greenan Mountain, or the nearby Elagh Castle. Recent excavations have made the latter a more likely candidate, and I have chosen to go along with that theory, though the Grianan was certainly an important place. I have it as a ceremonial site, much like the ancient site of Tara, which also fell into disuse but retained its status as a sacred coronation site.

The Irish lived within enclosures of many types—artificial islands (crannogs), forts with timber walls (raths), or stone walls (cashels). Some of the enclosures were for defense, but many seemed to be simply to keep livestock in or out. These enclosures were round and so were most of their buildings.

Currachs—these Irish boats were made of hide stretched over a structure of branches and sealed with tar. Small currachs, intended for lakes and rivers, were nearly round in shape, and sculled with a single paddle from the bow. Others were much larger, rowed or propelled by sail and quite seaworthy. There are ancient Irish legends of long sea voyages (immrama) in them— such as Saint Brendan, which may well have been based on an earlier pagan tale.

IRISH TERMS

- **A chroi**—my heart
- **A ghra**—my love
- **A mhuirin**—my darling
- **Ard Ri**—High king
- **Bard**—the poet class of Irish intellectual society
- **Bratt**—a wool wrap worn by both sexes
- **Brehon**—a legal expert of the Irish intellectual class
- **Cashel**—a fort with stone walls
- **Cenel**—kindred
- **Crannog**—an island fortress
- **Currach**—a boat made of cowhide stretched over a framework of branches. They can be large or small, the smaller ones sculled with a single paddle from the bow, the larger ones rowed.
- **Dun**—a stronghold
- **Filidh**—the intellectual class of Irish society, predating Christianity, comprised of druids, bards, and brehons
- **Finn gaill**—white foreigners (Norse)
- **Grianan**—palace of the sun
- **Leine**—a gown, worn by both men and women

- **Leite**—breakfast
- **Lochlainn**—Norway
- **Ollave**—the highest rank of bard
- **Rath**—a fort with earthen walls
- **Sil**—progeny
- **Sidhe**—the faerie folk of Ireland, who dwell in the mounds and are said to be the ancient Tuatha de Danann
- **Souterrain**—(French) underground rooms and passages used for escape and cold storage
- **Tuath**—clan or tribe

NORSE TERMS

- **Álf**—elf, male, often considered ancestors (plural álfir)
- **Berserker**—warriors said to have superhuman powers. Translates either as "bear shirt" or "bare shirt" (also berserk)
- **Bindrune**—three or more runes drawn one over the other
- **Blót**—sacrifice. i.e., Álfablót is sacrifice in honor of the elves, Dísablót is in honor of the dís
- **Bower**—women's quarters, usually a separate building
- **Breeks**—breeches
- **Brisingamen**—Golden necklace belonging to the goddess Freyja
- **Brynja**—chain-mail shirt
- **Dís**—spirits of female ancestors (plural: dísir)
- **Distaff**—a staff for holding unspun wool or linen fibers during the spinning process. About a meter long, usually made of wood or iron, with a bail to hold the wool. Historically associated with witchcraft.
- **Draugr**—animated corpse
- **Fylgja**—a guardian spirit, animal or female

- **Fóstra**—a child's nurse (foster mother)
- **Flyting**—a contest of insults
- **Galdr**—spells spoken and sung
- **Gammelost**—literally "old cheese"
- **Godi**—a priest
- **Gungnir**—Odin's spear
- **Hamr**—"skin"; the body
- **Haugbui**—mound-dwelling ghost
- **Haugr**—mound
- **Hird**—the warrior retinue of a noble – húskarlar
- **Holmgang**—"island-going"; a duel within boundaries
- **Hudfat**—sleeping bags made of sheepskin
- **Hugr**—the soul, the mind
- **Húskarl**—the elite household warriors of a nobleman (plural: húskarlar)
- **Jarl**—earl, one step below a king
- **Jól**—Yule midwinter feast honoring all the gods, but especially Odin
- **Karl**—a free man
- **Karvi**—a small Viking ship
- **Kenning**—a metaphorical expression in Old Norse poetry
- **Knarr**—a merchant ship
- **Lawspeaker**—a learned man who knew the laws of the district by heart
- **Longfire**—a long, narrow firepit that ran down the center of a hall
- **Mjölnir**—Thor's hammer, a symbol of fertility
- **Norn**—the supernatural sisters who weave fate named Skuld, Verdandi, and Urd
- **Odal land**—inherited land
- **Ørlög**—personal fate
- **Primstave**—a flat piece of wood used as a calendar.

The days of summer are carved on one side, winter on the reverse.

- **Ragnarök**—the final battle of the gods—the end of the world
- **Runes**—the Viking alphabet, said to have magical powers, also used in divination
- **Seidr**—a trance to work magic
- **Shield-maiden**—female warrior
- **Shield wall**—a battle formation
- **Skáld**—poet
- **Skagerrak Sea**—a body of water between Southeast Norway, Southwest Sweden, and Northern Denmark
- **Skerry**—a small rocky islet
- **Skutching**—scraping the flax stalk from the inner fibers
- **Skyr**—a dairy product similar to yogurt
- **Small beer**—a beer with a low alcohol content, a common drink
- **Steering oar or steering board**—a long oar that acted as a rudder. It was hung over the starboard side and attached to a tiller
- **Stook**—a group of sheaves stood on end in a field
- **Sverige, Svea**—Sweden and Swedes
- **Swine horn**—a v-shaped battle formation
- **Tafl**—also Hnefatafl, a chess-like board game found in Viking graves
- **Thrall**—slave
- **Tiercel**—a male falcon, usually smaller than the female
- **Ting, Allting**—assembly at which legal matters are settled
- **Ulfhed**—"wolf head"; another warrior like a berserker (plural ulfhednar)
- **Urdr**—(Anglo-Saxon *wyrd*) the web of fate, the name of one of the Norns

- **Valhöll**—"corpse hall," Odin's hall
- **Valknut**—"corpse knot," a symbol of Odin
- **Valkyrie**—"choosers of the slain," or corpse maidens. Magical women who take warriors from the battlefield to Valhöll, or Freyja's hall Folkvang
- **Vardlokkur**—a song to draw the spirits
- **Völva**—a sorceress. Literally, "wand-bearer"
- **Weregild**—the value of a person's life, to be paid in wrongful death
- **Wights**—spirits of land and water
- **Wootz**—crucible steel manufactured in ancient India

CHARACTERS

TROMØY—AN ISLAND OFF THE EAST COAST OF AGDER, NORWAY

- Åsa, age 19, queen of Tromøy, daughter of the murdered King Harald Redbeard
- Halfdan the Black, Åsa's three-year-old son
- Brenna, Halfdan's nurse (fóstra)
- Toki, Brenna's husband, steward of Tromøy
- Olvir, head of Åsa's household guards
- Jarl Borg of Iveland, Åsa's military advisor
- Ulf, blacksmith of Tromøy
- Heid, a famous völva (sorceress), Åsa's mentor
- Knut, a famous traveling skáld (poet and historian)
- Ragnhild Solvisdottir, age 17, leader of Tromøy's shield-maidens
- Einar, Thorgeir, Svein—warriors formerly of Solbakk, now sworn to Ragnhild
- Helga, (deceased) eldest of five sisters from a farm in Agder's hinterlands

- Unn, second eldest of Helga's sisters
- Alm, farm boy from Agder's hinterland
- Behrt, a displaced Christian warrior
- Sigrid, Heid's slave
- Stormrider, Åsa's peregrine falcon
- Flekk, Åsa's dog
- Harald Redbeard, King of East Agder, Norway, Åsa and Gyrd's father (deceased)
- Gunnhild, his queen, Åsa and Gyrd's mother, a noblewoman of Lista (deceased)
- Gyrd, their son, Åsa's brother (deceased)

VESTFOLD

Skiringssal, the Shining Hall of Vestfold, Norway
    Borre, another stronghold of Vestfold, north of Skiringssal

- Olaf, age 20, king of Vestfold, son of King Gudrød
- Sonja Eisteinsdottir, age 18, Olaf's wife
- Kalv, captain of Olaf's guard
- Gudrød, deceased king of Vestfold, Olaf's father, formerly Åsa's husband
- Alfhild, Gudrød's first wife, Olaf's mother (deceased)
- Halfdan the Mild, Gudrød's deceased father—Olaf's grandfather

SOLBAKK, ROGALAND

- Solvi, king
- Ragnhild, Solvi's daughter, age 17
- Harald Goldbeard, Solvi's eldest son, age 20
- Signy, daughter of the king of Sogn, Harald's' wife, age 17

- Orlyg, Solvi's younger son, age 18
- Katla, Ragnhild's foster mother

ORKNEY

- Ivar, the chieftain
- Gudrun, Ivar's wife
- Kol, a warrior

IRELAND

Note on spellings: In my research I discovered that Irish names have multiple spellings—I have chosen spellings and tried to be consistent. The pronunciation is complex—for example, Conchobar is pronounced Connor.

- Murchad mac Maele Duin, king of Aileach of the Northern Ui Neill—Cenel nEoghan
- Niall mac Aeda, Murchad's cousin and foster brother
- Aife, a brehon
- Fiona, maidservant of Aileach
- Ailesh, Maire, Orlath, other maidservants
- Father Ferdia, priest of Aileach
- Fergal, a stable boy
- Seamus, bard of Aileach
- Brunaidh, a pony

OTHERS

- Aed, chieftain of Tullynavin
- Diarmait mac Neill of Ui Chernaig, a branch of the Sil nAedo Slaine, part of the southern Ui Neill

- Conchobar mac Donnchada, king of Tara, of the Southern Ui Neill, Murchad's rival, self-proclaimed High King of Ireland
- Brother Brian, a hermit

MONASTERY OF DAIRE CALGACH

- Abbot Ennae
- Brother Padraig, gatekeeper
- Brother Oengus, blacksmith
- Brother Aidan, Oengus' assistant

NORSE GODS

- Odin—lord of the Aesir gods, of many names
- Valhöll—Odin's hall—literally, "corpse hall"
- Einherjar—heroes slain in battle who come to Valhöll
- Gungnir—Odin's spear that marks an army as his
- Sleipnir—Odin's horse
- Thor—Odin's son, god of thunder, preserver of mankind
- Mjölnir—Thor's hammer
- Freyja—originally of the Vanir gods. Goddess of love and magic. She gets first pick of the slain heroes for her hall her hall is Folkvang—"People's Field."
- Frey—Freyja's twin brother, fertility god of peace and plenty
- Loki—originally a giant, a trickster god
- Hel—Loki's daughter, mistress of the dead who don't fall in battle
- Nifleheim—cold and misty land of the dead, ruled by Hel

- Ran—goddess of the sea
- Yggdrasil—"Odin's steed", the world tree, that holds the nine worlds
- Norns—three sisters who spin the lives of men and gods

IRISH GODS AND HEROES

- Aine—goddess of summer
- Lugh—god of the sun
- Grainne—daughter of the king of Tara
- Diarmuid—Grianne's reluctant lover
- Finn Mac Cumhaill—Irish hero

ACKNOWLEDGMENTS

I have so many people to thank in bringing this novel into being: My beloved mother who first introduced me to Åsa and the Viking world; my wonderful fellow writers at Kitsap Writers, each of whom contributed so very much and kept me going; and to critique partners DV Berkom, Chris Karlsen, and Jennifer Conner. Thanks to my dear husband Brian who is always on my side and eager to read more, and beta readers Colleen Hogan-Taylor, Jay and Linda S., each of whom gave me priceless insights. I owe many thanks to editors Ruth Ross Saucier and Laurie Boris. Any errors that exist in this book are entirely my own.

ABOUT THE AUTHOR

Like her Viking forebears, Johanna Wittenberg has sailed to the far reaches of the world. She lives on a fjord in the Pacific Northwest with her husband, whom she met on a ship bound for Antarctica.

Website: https://JohannaWittenberg.com
    You can find her on social media at:

 facebook.com/TheNorseQueen
        twitter.com/JoWit5

Printed in Great Britain
by Amazon